CHRISTMAS AT LAKESIDE

A SWEET SMALL-TOWN ROMANCE

RETURN TO SAPPHIRE BAY, BOOK 4

LEEANNA MORGAN

ABOUT THIS BOOK

**"All the books in this series had me holding my breath
with each turn of a page. Five stars!"**

**Fans of Netflix's Virgin River series and Sweet Magnolias
will love this small-town, feel-good romance!**

Katie Terry loves her family, but she never wanted to return
to Sapphire Bay. After the twelve-month clause in her grandmother's will comes to an end, she's moving back to Los
Angeles to pursue her dream of becoming a bestselling
author.

Peter Bennett has made a fortune developing IT solutions
that change people's lives. His latest project, a 3D prosthetic
limb, is creating world-wide interest. Leaving New York
City behind, he travels to Sapphire Bay to evaluate the clinical trials and secure funding to commercially produce the
state-of-the-art invention.

When he meets Katie, he's intrigued by her heartfelt desire to
make the world a better place—one book at a time. As their
lives become more entwined, he can't help but wonder what
it would be like to live with someone who sees sunshine in
the darkest of days. But her big city dreams are pulling her
away and he doesn't know if what they have is strong enough
to make her want to stay.

CHRISTMAS AT LAKESIDE is the fourth book in the Return to Sapphire Bay series that follows the Terry sisters as they return to a community with big hearts and warm smiles. Romance, adventure, and intrigue are waiting for you in Sapphire Bay!

If you would like to know when my next book is released, please visit leeannamorgan.com and sign up for my newsletter. Happy reading!

FOREWORD

On November 19, 1863, President Abraham Lincoln
delivered a speech in Gettysburg, Pennsylvania that would
become one of the best-known speeches in American
history.

This book is dedicated to everyone who strives to create a
world where all men are created equal.

The Gettysburg Address

The following speech is the Bliss copy of the Gettysburg Address and is in the public
domain. The text is original to the 1863 speech, including any spelling and grammatical
issues we would have changed in the twenty-first century :)

Four score and seven years ago our fathers brought forth on
this continent, a new nation, conceived in Liberty, and dedicated to the proposition that all men are created equal.

Now we are engaged in a great civil war, testing whether that
nation, or any nation so conceived and so dedicated, can
long endure. We are met on a great battle-field of that war.

We have come to dedicate a portion of that field, as a final resting place for those who here gave their lives that that nation might live. It is altogether fitting and proper that we should do this.

But, in a larger sense, we can not dedicate—we can not consecrate—we can not hallow—this ground. The brave men, living and dead, who struggled here, have consecrated it, far above our poor power to add or detract. The world will little note, nor long remember what we say here, but it can never forget what they did here. It is for us the living, rather, to be dedicated here to the unfinished work which they who fought here have thus far so nobly advanced. It is rather for us to be here dedicated to the great task remaining before us—that from these honored dead we take increased devotion to that cause for which they gave the last full measure of devotion—that we here highly resolve that these dead shall not have died in vain—that this nation, under God, shall have a new birth of freedom—and that government of the people, by the people, for the people, shall not perish from the earth.

Abraham Lincoln
November 19, 1863.

CHAPTER 1

Katie sat at the kitchen table in The Lakeside Inn, anxiously waiting for her sisters to join her. Each Monday evening, they met to discuss what was happening at their Bed and Breakfast over the following week.

Apart from welcoming new guests, the next few weeks would be super-busy. With her sister Penny's Thanksgiving Day wedding behind them, they had another sister's wedding to look forward to.

Diana was marrying Ethan on Christmas Eve in a fairy forest in the center of Sapphire Bay. With chocolate fountains, crystal chandeliers, and thousands of lights strung through the trees and flowers, it was the most romantic venue Katie could imagine.

"Sorry I'm late. How long have you been waiting?" Barbara's laptop banged against the table as she sat opposite Katie.

"Only for a few minutes. Where's Penny and Diana?"

"They'll be here soon. Penny texted me a few minutes ago to say they were about to leave Sweet Treats."

"They've probably sampled every cake flavor in the store."

"Probably." Barbara smiled as Charlie, their lovable Golden Labrador, walked into the kitchen and flopped at her feet. "At least they didn't take Charlie. His nose wouldn't have stopped twitching at all the delicious scents."

Katie glanced at her cell phone.

"Is everything okay?"

"My agent's emailing a publishing contract to me."

"That's amazing! Why didn't you tell me sooner?"

Katie sighed. Her family had been incredibly supportive of her efforts to become a published children's author, but there were only so many rejections anyone could handle. "I didn't want everyone to get excited in case it amounts to nothing."

"It's never nothing. Even though no one has offered you a contract until now, you've been given some valuable advice."

She didn't say anything. Being told repeatedly that she was a talented author didn't make up for not having any published books. If the editors really thought she was amazing, they would have snapped up her manuscripts by now.

Charlie's ears pricked up and he rushed toward the front door.

"Penny and Diana must be home," Katie said as she followed him into the hallway.

Opening the front door, she stood on the veranda with her jacket wrapped firmly around her. As she watched her sisters walk toward the inn, she couldn't help but remember what had brought them back to Sapphire Bay. Seven months ago, their beloved Grandma had died. In her will, she'd left her home to her four granddaughters with one condition. They had to live here for a year. Otherwise, the home would be given to the church for emergency housing.

Out of all her sisters, she and Barbara were the least excited about living in Montana. It wasn't that they didn't love the small town, because they did. They were born and raised here, enjoying an idyllic childhood on the shore of Flathead Lake. But college and their careers had taken them to other parts of the States. She'd moved to Los Angeles and Barbara had made her home in San Diego. After their grandma died it had taken a lot of coercion but, eventually, they'd both agreed to stay.

With no income and limited employment opportunities, Katie had remodeled their grandparents' home with her sisters and opened a Bed and Breakfast. The additional income was a welcome relief and meeting their guests was better than anyone imagined.

But all good things had to end. Even though she was enjoying her time with her family, in five months she would move back to Los Angeles. If she was ever going to be a published author, she needed to be close to her agent, and close to where the publishing houses had offices.

Katie smiled as Charlie raced across the yard. "How were the wedding cake samples?" she asked her sisters.

Diana lifted a large bag in the air. "You can taste them for yourself. Megan gave us some to bring home."

Charlie was already wagging his tail, following the movement of the bag as if he hadn't eaten in days.

"It's okay, boy," Diana said softly. "We stopped at Mom and Dad's store and bought you some treats."

Penny took a brown paper bag out of her pocket. Without missing a beat, Charlie switched his allegiance and looked pleadingly at her.

"How can I resist those big, brown doggy eyes?" Reaching into the bag, she handed him a chewy treat.

"I wish you were that well-behaved on our walks," Katie said as he climbed the steps with his treasure.

As if knowing exactly what she'd said, Charlie looked at her with his eyes full of mischief. The only way he'd stop running into the lake was if she filled her pockets with yummy treats.

Diana walked into the kitchen and sighed. "It's a lot warmer in here." Taking two small boxes out of the bag, she handed one to Katie. "This cake's for you. It's caramel deluxe."

"Yum."

"And for Barbara, we have vanilla cream and huckleberry swirl."

"That sounds divine."

"It's Ethan's favorite." Diana took the last two boxes out of the bag. She handed one to Penny and left the other one on the counter.

Penny made everyone a cup of coffee. "I'm glad it's your turn to get married. It's much less stressful being a brides-maid than a bride."

Katie's cell phone pinged.

Barbara looked at her. "Is that your agent?"

Penny and Diana looked at each other.

"What does she want?" Penny asked.

Katie's heart sank at Penny's hopeful expression. "Nalini's emailing a contract for me to review."

Diana's eyes widened. "And you didn't tell us?"

"It's not one hundred percent guaranteed. The publishing house was still considering my manuscript when she last spoke to them." Katie opened the email and wished she hadn't.

Barbara took one look at Katie and sighed. "Are you okay?"

Taking a deep breath, she plastered a smile on her face. After too many rejections to count, there was no point getting upset. "I'm all right. The publishing house loved my manuscript, but it isn't what they're looking for."

"That's crazy," Diana spluttered. "You're a wonderful writer."

"It's okay. Let's forget about the email and talk about the inn. What's happening this week?"

Barbara gave her a hug. "You're fierce as well as courageous. Don't let the email get you down."

"I won't." Regardless of what she'd said, a heavy weight settled on her shoulders. It didn't matter how many times she told herself the rejection letters didn't matter—they did. All she'd ever wanted to do was write stories for children. She'd spent three years studying creative writing, honing her skills until she was ready to submit her best manuscripts to agents. With more enthusiasm than was healthy, she'd naively thought the editors from every major publishing house would want to buy her books. But that hadn't happened.

Her parents and sisters had done so well in their chosen careers. But, here she was, still struggling to publish a book after years of trying. Even for someone who was usually positive, the constant stream of rejection letters made her feel like a failure.

Diana sat at the table. "I have some news that will take your mind off the email. If everyone's happy for Ethan to look after our guests, we can visit my friend in Kalispell on Wednesday."

Katie's imagination leaped to her sister's Christmas Eve wedding. Originally, Diana wanted a fairy theme, but that changed when Ethan saw what he'd be wearing.

Instead, they chose a Christmas theme and, to add a touch of whimsy to the occasion, the bridal party was renting their dresses from a theatrical company.

Barbara bit into her slice of cake. "Is your friend able to put some costumes aside for us? With all the Christmas parties happening, they might not have any dresses left by the time we get there."

"We discussed that this afternoon. She'll hang a few of her nicest ones in a special storage area for us. Mom and Dad are coming, too."

While everyone was enjoying their cake and coffee, Barbara opened her laptop. "We'd better start our meeting. The first item on the agenda is our guests."

As they talked about the bookings and the specific requests each couple had made, Katie tried not to think about the email. She had a lot to be grateful for, and at the top of the list was her family.

Another rejection letter wouldn't make her any less determined to publish her stories—even if it took her until she was eighty years old.

PETER LEANED back in his office chair and stretched. The view of Flathead Lake from his friend Zac's house was stunning. Even with a blanket of snow covering the surrounding mountains, everything looked fresh and crisp and almost too good to be true. It was a lot better than the concrete jungle he'd left behind in New York City.

"How's the report?"

He turned around and smiled at Zac. They'd met at a conference many years ago when they were beginning their medical careers. Zac was a young doctor, full of enthusiasm and ideas for improving the life of veterans. Peter had started his own biomedical company, doing his part in providing cutting-edge, high-tech solutions to medical issues that plagued people from all walks of life.

Even though they now lived hundreds of miles apart, they'd remained good friends. "I wish I could say the report's nearly done, but I can't. At least I'm closer to finishing it than I was last week."

"Did you get the results from the last two trial patients?"

"They'll be here this afternoon." Three years ago, his company started developing a product called an Interactive Neurological Prosthetic. Made from an advanced composite gel, the prosthetic molded to each patient's stump to create a perfect fit. But comfort was only a small part of the gel's ground-breaking benefits. Acting as a neural-conductor, the gel sent information from the brain to the limb, helping the prosthetic to move like a normal part of the human body.

The first steps in its development hadn't been easy.

After a huge amount of financial investment and rigorous clinical trials, Peter was finally at the stage where he was happy with the product they'd developed. But to take it farther, to bring the state-of-the-art prosthetic into a commercial market, would require even more money. Without the report, there would be no additional funding. The project would come to a standstill and thousands of amputees wouldn't have access to the life-changing prosthetic.

Peter handed Zac a copy of a chart he'd compiled.

His friend's eyebrows rose. "These results are better than you expected."

"I was worried we'd lose some of the responsiveness, especially after the last round of modifications."

"What's the worst that can happen with this design?"

"The limbs will look slightly different, but they'll cost half of what we initially thought."

"That sounds like the sort of trade-off most people can live with."

Peter frowned at the pile of folders stacked on the side of the desk. "I hope so. I had a call from Dave McCauley at

7

NASA. They've heard about our project and want to look at ways we can work together."

Zac crossed his arms in front of his chest. "How much do they know?"

"I'm not sure, but I'm keen to find out. All our trial recipients signed non-disclosure statements. No one except you, the amputees, and the research and development team should know about the project."

"There was always a risk someone would talk."

"I just wish they hadn't said anything for a few more months. At least we patented the technology as soon as it looked promising. Anyone wanting to copy our design will have a fight on their hands."

"I hope for your sake it doesn't come to that." Zac glanced through the window. "It's a great day. Do you want to go for a run? Willow and Tiffany are visiting some friends and it could be my last chance to get away."

Peter checked his watch. "Maybe next time. I have to go into town to collect some supplies. Can I get you anything?"

"Not at the moment. We've got everything we need."

With one last look at the pile of work sitting on his desk, Peter stood and grabbed his jacket. "If I was looking for a Christmas cake for you and Willow, where would I go?"

"You can't beat Megan's cakes at Sweet Treats, but you don't have to buy anything. We're enjoying having you here."

"We haven't seen much of each other since I arrived."

"That's because you're busy. Once the report's done, you can relax and enjoy the mountains and lake."

Peter grinned. "I can't remember the last time I wasn't thinking about work. How do you switch off your brain?"

"You get away from the rat race and live somewhere like Sapphire Bay. I can guarantee by the middle of January, you won't want to go back to New York."

Peter held out his hand. "That's too easy. Twenty bucks says I'll be ready to leave before then."

Zac shook his hand. "Done, but don't say I didn't warn you."

KATIE RAN her hands along a roll of tinsel and smiled. She'd always loved visiting her parents' general store at Christmas. Her mom, Mabel, loved anything and everything to do with the festive season. As well as selling pretty decorations and gifts made by the residents of Sapphire Bay, there were colorful displays of power tools, building materials, and DIY necessities—all covered in tinsel and Christmas baubles. Even the Christmas music playing softly in the background gave the store a festive spirit.

The workroom door opened and her dad walked through to the front of the store holding a large box.

Mabel appeared from behind him. "Over here, Allan. It needs to go beside the power tools."

"But it's a sewing machine. It should go with the ladies Christmas ideas."

"It has a motor. It goes with the power tools."

Katie smiled as her dad sighed. After forty years of marriage, he'd learned to pick his battles—and the placement of a sewing machine wasn't worth the effort it took to disagree with his wife.

Mabel looked across the store and saw Katie. With a wide smile, she beckoned her forward. "Come and have a look at this amazing sewing and quilting machine. A friend bought one last week and I had to have one in the store. Isn't it a beauty?"

Katie held the bottom of the box while her dad lifted the machine onto a table. "It's big."

"But not too big," Mabel assured her. "It has more than fourteen thousand five-star reviews on Amazon. If anyone in town wants a reasonably priced gift for a sewing enthusiast, this will do nicely."

Allan slid the empty box under the table and let the Christmas-themed tablecloth drop into place to hide it. "What brings you into town today, Katie? I thought you'd be writing."

She gave her mom and dad a hug. "Everyone liked how I decorated the inn for Thanksgiving, so I've been given the job of decorating it for Christmas. I found a lot of things in the garage, but I need more tinsel, a tree, and something special for our guests' bedrooms."

The doorbell jingled as Mabel reached for Katie's hand. "Come with me. Your dad added more tinsel to our display this morning."

A man in a blue ski jacket and black beanie walked into the store.

Katie didn't think she'd seen him around town. "I can wait if you want to serve the person who came into the store."

"Your dad will help him."

Allan smiled at his wife. "Anything for you, my love." And with a wink, he walked across to the stranger.

Katie followed her mom to the other side of the room. At least a dozen different shades of tinsel were hanging from the shelves. "These are lovely. I didn't know you could get peach colored tinsel."

"Neither did I until I saw them in the catalog. What colors are you using to decorate the inn?"

Tilting her head to the side, Katie considered her options. "Grandma used to decorate the house in gold and red, but I'd like a rainbow of colors. Can I buy three rolls of each color?"

"Of course, you can."

Katie looked around for a basket. With that many rolls, she was bound to drop something on the floor.

"Are you looking for one of these?" her dad asked.

"I was. Thanks." She took the basket and added as much tinsel as she could without leaving the stand bare. While she was hanging it on the inn's walls, she'd have to be careful not to leave it dangling where Charlie, their goofy Golden Lab, could pull it down and eat it.

Her dad reached around her shoulders and took two rolls of green tinsel off the display. "I'd better take these before they're all gone. Have you met, Peter, Katie? He's staying with Zac for a few weeks."

Katie automatically smiled at the visitor who was standing behind her dad. His blue eyes connected with hers and, for a few seconds, she forgot where she was. Her mom cleared her throat, jarring Katie out of her brain freeze.

Standing taller, she held out her hand. "It's nice to meet you."

Peter returned her smile. "Nice to meet you, too. You have a lot of tinsel in your basket."

Katie's hand tightened on the handle. "I'll probably need more before I've finished. I have a big house to decorate."

"Willow and Zac have already decorated their home, but I thought I'd add a little more Christmas cheer to the office where I'm working."

Katie looked at the tinsel her dad was holding. "You can't go wrong with green tinsel."

"That's what I thought."

Peter took off his beanie and Katie's breath caught. With his short, dark hair and clear blue eyes, he was handsome in an understated way. The kind of way that could be dangerous to a woman who hadn't dated anyone in more than a year.

"I was just telling Peter about the store at the Christmas

11

Tree Farm," her dad said. "He's looking for some ornaments he can take back to New York for his family."

Mabel added another couple of rolls of tinsel to Katie's basket. "They have some lovely handmade crafts. It's definitely worth visiting. Are you getting your tree from there, Katie?"

She glanced at her mom. "I'm going there next. A friend went to the farm yesterday and said the trees are selling much faster than last year."

"If Peter wants some special ornaments, he could follow you in his vehicle," Mabel said far too sweetly. "If the trees are selling like hotcakes, so will the ornaments."

While Katie couldn't fault her mom's logic, she was a little worried about her motivation. "Peter probably has other things he'd rather do." She looked into his amused blue eyes. "I could draw a map showing you how to get there."

"A map won't do," Mabel said. "Peter could drive straight past the entrance."

Considering all the signage on the road, the likelihood of that happening was as remote as an iceberg suddenly appearing on Flathead Lake.

Mabel smiled at Peter. "It's always better when someone takes you to a new place, especially in Montana. Everything is so spread out compared to what you must be used to."

Peter's eyes crinkled at the corners.

Katie got the impression he knew exactly what her mom was up to. "If you're leaving soon, I'm happy to follow you."

"That's perfect," Mabel said enthusiastically. "You won't be disappointed."

His smile turned into a grin. "I'm sure I won't."

With her dad hurrying away to serve another customer, Mabel took them both to the front counter. Katie hoped her mom wasn't playing matchmaker. Just because her sisters had found their happy-ever-afters since they'd returned to Sapphire Bay, it didn't mean she was looking for hers.

CHAPTER 2

*A*s soon as he drove under the red and gold sign welcoming visitors to The Christmas Tree Farm, Peter rolled down his window. The clean, fresh scent of pine filled his lungs and made him appreciate being away from the smog and pollution of New York City.

Keeping a steady pace behind Katie's truck, he eased his foot off the accelerator. With snow covering the trees on either side of the driveway, and a barn rising high into the sky, he was filled with a sense of rightness.

When he'd told his team he was going to Sapphire Bay to assess the progress of one of the trial participants, they'd thought he was crazy. There were plenty of other people who could have flown here but, each time he returned, he felt more content than he had in a long time.

Maybe that's why meeting Katie had left him feeling so off-center. For the first time in years, he was intrigued by a woman. And not just any woman. Katie was a petite red-head with pretty blue eyes and a mouth that refused to do anything other than smile.

When her mom suggested he follow her out to the farm,

she'd silently pleaded with him not to listen, but he *did* need gifts for his family. Even if she wasn't thrilled with her mom's offer, he was grateful. Getting lost had become one of his most successful pastimes. Whether it was in a mall's parking lot or on the main street of Sapphire Bay, he often forgot where he'd left his truck or how to get to his next destination. At least this way he hadn't ended up in the middle of nowhere.

As he followed the gravel driveway up to the red barn, his eyebrows rose. Katie wasn't exaggerating when she'd said it would be busy. At least thirty trucks were vying for position in the large front yard. And, from the left-hand side of the property, a line of vehicles carrying Christmas trees slowly made its way toward the main road.

He parked beside Katie and jumped out of his truck. When he opened her driver's door, her startled face lifted to his.

"You didn't have to do that."

"Mom told me it isn't polite to let a woman open a door if I can do it for her."

A soft blush swept across Katie's cheeks. "Well, that's very sweet. Thank you." She stepped out of the truck and watched the people walking into the Christmas shop. "This is the best Christmas store I've ever seen. As well as selling award-winning Christmas trees, Ben and Kylie sell a lot of hand-crafted ornaments. Most of them are made by the people who live around Flathead Lake. You won't find anything this good anywhere in the United States."

"That's high praise. I can't wait to go inside." And he truly couldn't. Judging by the smiles on people's faces as they returned to their vehicles, everyone seemed excited about what they'd seen.

As they walked through the large barn doors, Peter's surprise turned to amazement. It was hard to imagine a more impressive Christmas shop. The wall in front of him was painted bright red and covered in Christmas art. Fairy lights hung from the impossibly high rafters, cascading down the walls and twinkling from above the wooden shelves.

Everywhere he looked, people were picking up the merchandise and adding it to their baskets. "You weren't kidding when you said the shop's popular."

Katie moved out of the way of a young girl racing after a little boy. "You should be here on a Saturday or a Sunday. It's twice as hectic. Do you have any ideas about what you'd like to buy for your family?"

"My sister collects ornamental birds and Mom likes anything sparkly. I have no idea what to buy Dad."

"I have the same problem. Finding gifts for my mom and sisters is easy, but Dad's impossible. I saw some lovely ornaments on the far side of the store last week. Come with me."

Before Peter knew what she was doing, Katie grabbed his hand and pulled him down an aisle. Her hand was warm and small inside of his and made his heart beat a little faster. With that kind of reaction, he really needed to meet more people instead of spending so much time at work.

"They're over here, beside the quilts."

His gaze roamed over shelves full of colorful crafts and decorations. He could easily spend an hour here and still not see everything.

Katie stopped and he nearly ran into her back.

"What do you think?" She looked up at him and smiled. "If your mom likes bling, she'll love these baubles."

Reluctantly, he pulled his gaze away from Katie and saw the bright red glass ball she was holding. Imbedded in the glass were hundreds of shiny beads, glittering like stars under the old-fashioned pendant lights hanging above them.

"They're fifteen dollars each, but you wouldn't need to buy lots of them. They come in a nice box and the staff will gift-wrap what you buy. You even have the option of engraving a message on the glass."

He smiled and took the decoration out of Katie's hands. "You should work here."

"That's what Kylie, Ben's wife, said. But between the inn and my writing, I'm too busy."

"The inn?"

"The Lakeside Inn. My grandma died seven months ago and left her home to my sisters and me. The only condition was that we had to live in the house together for a year." She moved out of the way of another shopper. "Moving from Los Angeles wasn't an easy decision, but it's worked out for the best."

Sapphire Bay was spectacular, but he couldn't imagine living here if he hadn't made the decision himself.

Katie handed him a basket. "Use this. It'll make shopping easier." She looked over her shoulder and waved at a man walking toward her. "That's Ben, the owner of The Christmas Tree Farm. Are you okay shopping on your own or do you want some help?"

Peter was tempted to ask her to stay, but she'd already spent more time with him than she needed to. "It's all right. I'm happy to look around on my own."

Katie's dimpled grin made him sigh. "If you don't find what you want, we have an amazing Christmas market in town in a couple of weeks."

"I'll keep that in mind."

She held out her hand, and the same odd feeling of rightness snuck up on him. "Bye, Peter. I might see you around town some time."

As she joined the owner of the farm, he flexed his tingling fingers. If he'd had an ounce of common sense, he would have asked Katie if she wanted to meet for coffee. But he hadn't and it was too late.

It was just as well his friend Zac knew most of the people in town. He was bound to know where he could find The Lakeside Inn. And if he didn't, there was always the Internet.

KATIE TOOK a deep breath and felt the magical power of the Christmas tree plantation wash over her. This was her favorite time of the year, the time when wishes came true and most people found something to be happy about.

When she was a little girl, her parents brought her sisters and grandparents to the farm to choose their Christmas trees. It was only open for a few months each year, so it was a treat to be here.

Since Ben had bought the property, the farm had become a year-round tourist destination. When he wasn't selling trees, his store supported local artists and crafts people by selling Christmas-themed decorations and art. She still couldn't believe how popular the farm had become, especially after Ben told her how difficult the first few years had been.

Today, Ben was helping her choose the perfect tree for the inn. Sitting on the back of his four-wheeler was so much easier than trudging through the snow.

He pointed to the trees on their right-hand side. "The Scots Pine are about 14 feet tall. What do you think?"

He brought the four-wheeler to a standstill and Katie jumped off the back. Standing beside the trees, she tried to imagine one of them in the inn's living room. "They're perfect. If they were any shorter, they'd be swallowed by the size of the room."

"They're a good size and shape for what you're looking for. Is there one you like better than the others?"

This was the part she liked the best. With a spring in her

step, she made her way down the snow-covered row of trees. Her boots scrunched against the ground and occasionally she slipped, but she didn't care. Her sisters had trusted her to choose the centerpiece of their Christmas decorations, and she wouldn't let them down.

One of the trees caught her eye. Standing a little taller than the others, it was greeting card perfect. "I like this one."

Ben nodded. "Good choice. I'll get my chainsaw and call for a truck. It won't take too long to get it back to the store."

Katie waited patiently while he felled the tree and helped his staff load it into their truck. With other staff doing the same thing, the whole process of getting the trees from the farm to the store was seamless and efficient.

When Ben was ready to leave the tree-lined area of the farm, Katie pulled on her motorcycle helmet. "Thanks for coming here with me. I know how busy you are."

"It was no problem. Besides, Kylie wanted me to help you. You and your sisters buy a lot of flowers for the inn from her store."

"That's because she's an amazing florist. I can't wait to show my sisters the tree."

Ben smiled. "On that happy note, let's head back to the parking lot. Will someone be at the inn to help you get it inside?"

"There should be but, if not, I'll call Ethan and Wyatt. They'll help." Katie climbed onto the back of the four-wheeler and breathed a sigh of relief. With the tree organized, all she had to do was cover it in lights, tinsel, and decorations to make it look even more amazing than it was.

AFTER SPENDING MORE time at The Christmas Tree Farm than he should have, Peter drove back into town. As he climbed out of his truck, he looked across the parking lot at the tiny home village. Twenty homes, built as permanent accommodation for people who used to be homeless, filled a large lot opposite The Connect Church.

From conception to the grand opening, the village had taken more than two years to complete. It was only through hard work and perseverance that Pastor John and the community had managed to build something that was making a huge difference in many people's lives.

If it hadn't been for Richard, one of the residents, joining the clinical trial for the prosthetic limbs, he might never have appreciated just how special it was.

"Hi, Mr. Bennett."

He turned and smiled at Richard's seven-year-old son. "How are you, Jack?"

"I'm doing great. So is Dad."

Picking up his laptop and a box, he joined Jack on the sidewalk. "I like your sled."

The grin that lit his face made Peter smile, too. "Thanks. Pastor John found it for me. Do you want to come for a ride?"

"Not on this visit, but I'll keep it in mind for next time. Is your dad home?"

"He's at the church helping Pastor John get ready for a meeting. I'm going to see him, too."

"I'll follow you, then."

Jack nodded solemnly. "Dad's leg is good. He said it's better than a real one, but I like my legs."

Peter's lips twitched. "I'm glad. How's school?"

"It's okay. We're making things for the Christmas market. My teacher said it's an opportunity to show people how talented we are."

Peter smiled at the pride in the boy's voice. "That sounds like a fun thing to do."

"It is, except my friend Nora wants to bake Christmas muffins and my teacher said we can't. I hope she changes her mind because Nora's aunt makes the best cakes ever." Jack dropped his sled on the ground and opened the back door. "Dad's in here." After stomping his feet on the doormat, he hurried down the hallway.

The church and The Welcome Center were like a home away from home for Jack and his dad. From what Richard had told him, they'd arrived in Sapphire Bay with nothing except the clothes on their backs and Pastor John's name.

John had found them beds in The Welcome Center, given them a hot meal, and started the slow process of helping them emerge from the tragic situation they'd found themselves in.

Jack walked into one of the meeting rooms and ran up to his dad. "I found Mr. Bennett in the parking lot."

Richard looked over his son's head and smiled. "Hi, Peter. It's good to see you."

He shook Richard's hand. "It's good to see you, too."

Jack looked at his dad. "Are you going to do your exercises for Mr. Bennett?"

"That's the plan." Richard looked around the room. "All I have to do is add another six chairs to the back row and we can leave."

With an efficiency that wouldn't have been possible eighteen months ago, Richard lifted the chairs out of a storage area and placed them beside the others. Peter tried not to look as though he was evaluating Richard, but it was hard not to focus on the response of his leg in relation to the movement of the rest of his body.

After he'd finished, Richard turned to Peter and smiled. "Did I pass the Peter Bennett real-world test?"

"With flying colors. Have you had any issues with your leg?"

"None that I can recall. I downloaded the latest software like you asked me to. Did it help your staff in New York?"

"It was great. The data we collect will help us refine the program even more than the last time."

Pastor John walked into the room pushing a cart. When he saw Peter, he smiled. "I thought you'd be arriving soon. Did Richard tell you he's now the foreman of one of our construction teams?"

Peter's eyebrows rose. Richard had been working at the old steamboat museum for months, creating tiny homes for communities across Montana. "You didn't tell me you're one of the bosses."

The big man with a bushy beard and shoulders as wide as a doorway, blushed. "I'm still getting used to it."

"We couldn't have taken on another contract without you." John looked around the meeting room. "Thanks for organizing the room while you waited for Peter."

"It was no problem."

John smiled and looked at Jack. "How about having after-noon tea with me while your dad talks to Mr. Bennett?"

"Can we make chocolate milkshakes?"

"We can definitely make milkshakes." John lifted his gaze to Richard and Peter. "After you've finished, if we're not in the kitchen, we'll be with the other children in the after school program."

Richard ruffled his son's red hair. "Be good."

"I will." And with a happy smile, he left the meeting room with John.

Peter picked up his laptop and the box he'd brought inside. "How does it feel to be doing our last evaluation?"

"A little overwhelming. I'm incredibly grateful I was even on the trial team. The prosthetic leg has changed my life."

"I'm glad you were part of the team. Are we working from the same room we usually do?"

With a nod, Richard held open the door. "After we've finished, I'll introduce you to Nathaniel. He moved to Sapphire Bay a few weeks ago."

Peter didn't have to ask if he was an amputee. Richard was on a mission to get as many people as possible using the prosthetics. But with phase one at an end, no one would be receiving new limbs if Peter couldn't find any funders. And that, beyond anything else, would be heartbreaking.

CHAPTER 3

*K*atie stood back from the Christmas tree and frowned. "It needs something else, but I'm not sure what."

Penny tilted her head to the side. "We couldn't hang more tinsel from the branches, even if we wanted to."

Diana rescued a pink, glittery ball from Charlie's paws.

Their Golden Lab loved decorating the tree. Since they'd started, he'd hovered beside the boxes of decorations, waiting for something to fall on the floor as they'd opened them. So far, they'd only had to rescue six-feet of tinsel and three sparkly balls from his clutches.

After Diana attached the pink ball to the tree, she studied the branches. "Before we decide what it needs, let's turn on the fairy lights."

"Good idea." Katie picked up the plug.

"Watch your head," Penny warned as she crawled under the tree.

Dipping her head lower, she managed to steer clear of the lower branches. With a satisfying click, she pushed the plug into the socket. "What does it look like?"

Penny's sigh said it all. "It's gorgeous."

Katie wiggled out from under the tree. Her sister was right. With its shiny baubles and fluffy balls of spray-on snow, it was wonderful.

Diana returned a decoration to its box. "We don't need anything else. It's big, it's bold, and it's beautiful."

Katie rearranged a piece of tinsel on a branch. "Our guests will love it."

"Talking about our guests," Penny said. "Are the Donaldsons back from town yet?"

"They're still shopping." Diana picked up an empty box. "I'm meeting them at Cassie's jewelry store in an hour."

When the doorbell rang, Charlie ran across the room, his tail wagging happily.

"I'll get it," Katie told her sisters. She followed Charlie into the entryway, wondering who it could be. She just hoped it wasn't a history buff wanting to see the replica dresser in their living room. With everything turned topsy-turvy while they were decorating the tree, it wasn't the best time to ask about the letter they'd found.

When she opened the door, she smiled at their unexpected visitor. "Hi, Peter."

"Hi. I didn't mean to interrupt, but I saw the sign for the inn and thought I'd come and say hello." He bent down and gave Charlie's back a rub. "Who's this?"

"That's Charlie." Katie laughed when their big, cuddly, canine buddy leaned into Peter's legs. "He'll never be a guard dog, but we don't mind. Would you like to come inside? I was just about to make everyone a cup of coffee."

"Thanks. That would be great." He wiped his feet on the doormat and followed her inside. "Are many people staying here at the moment?"

"We have a full house." Katie stopped in the middle of

the living room. "You'll have to excuse the mess. While our guests are sightseeing, we thought we'd decorate the tree."

Diana and Penny looked up from what they were doing.

If Penny's raised eyebrows were anything to go by, she was as surprised as Katie to see their visitor.

"Peter, I'd like you to meet my sisters. Diana's on the left and Penny's on the right-hand side of the tree."

He nodded at the two women. "It's nice to meet you. I'm Peter Bennett. I met Katie in the general store."

"And then he followed me to The Christmas Tree Farm." Katie hurried across the room and rescued another decoration from Charlie.

When Penny's eyebrows rose again, Peter grinned. "I followed your sister for all the right reasons. I was looking for some gifts for my family and your mom suggested the Christmas shop."

Penny smiled. "That makes more sense. Are you staying in Sapphire Bay for long?"

"Not as long as I'd like. I'm going home in January."

"Well, at least you can enjoy Sapphire Bay until then."

Katie picked up the old tinsel that was destined for the trash. "Who wants coffee?"

Penny shook her head. "Not for me. I have a meeting in town."

"I'll have one," Diana said as she picked up three boxes. "I just need to take the decorations we aren't using to the garage."

Peter held out his hands. "I'm happy to help, too."

"Thanks. That would be great."

With a woof, Charlie joined Diana and Peter as they headed toward the front door.

"I'll have fresh coffee ready for you when you get back," Katie said.

Peter looked over his shoulder and smiled. "Sounds good."

And with his smile lingering in her mind, Katie walked into the kitchen. She didn't know what it was about him but, for someone she'd only just met, being around Peter was easy. If she didn't know better, she would have sworn she'd known him forever.

THE KITCHEN at The Lakeside Inn was every bit as grand as the entranceway and living room. Bathed in sunlight, the white cabinets and counter were the perfect backdrop for the amazing view of Flathead Lake. Peter couldn't imagine a more perfect location for a Bed and Breakfast.

As he sat at the kitchen table listening to Katie and Diana, he saw just how different they were. Diana was a lot quieter than Katie. She carefully considered what she said and let her sister do most of the talking. Katie was the complete opposite. With curly red hair and a restless energy, she was happy to answer any questions he asked. As she spoke, her hands moved in time with her words and her eyes gleamed with excitement. But when Diana mentioned something about her writing, the extrovert bursting out of Katie disappeared.

He took another sip of his coffee, choosing his next words carefully in case she changed the subject. "What type of stories do you write?"

Katie wrapped her hands around her mug. "I've written six children's books. They're about a group of friends who have all sorts of adventures."

"They're wonderful," Diana added. "Even children who find it hard to concentrate love listening to Katie's stories."

"Do you write under your own name or use a pen name?"

"I haven't published any of them, yet. But, when I do, I'll

use my own name. My agent has been trying to sell the manuscripts, but no one's interested in buying them."

Diana sighed. "It's almost as if you have to be someone famous like David Walliams or J.K. Rowling to be offered a contract."

Katie sat taller in her chair. "I understand why they've said no, even though it's disappointing. If you're a publishing house, you have a lot of expenses. If they accept an unknown author's manuscripts, they need to be sure they'll sell enough books to cover their costs. I guess they're not willing to take that risk."

"They'll never know until they try," Diana said stubbornly.

"Why don't you self-publish your stories?" he asked.

"That's what my sisters keep telling me," Katie murmured.

Diana bit into her cookie. "But you aren't listening."

"It's not that I'm absolutely opposed to publishing my own books. I just wouldn't have a clue where to start."

"Are there any online tutorials or workshops you could try?" Peter wasn't sure what the process involved, but a lot of other authors were publishing their own stories. "Someone must have documented a step-by-step process."

Katie frowned. "I found a couple of online workshops that had good reviews."

Diana smiled at Peter. "You should come here more often. That's the first time Katie's told us she's looked at anything to do with self-publishing."

"I'm keeping my options open, even if it doesn't look like it."

Peter saw the pride in Katie's eyes. He knew what it felt like to get a long way into a project then hit a brick wall. Sometimes, all it took was a fresh perspective to make the wall a little easier to climb. "I don't know anything about self-publishing, but I know my way around a computer. If you want me to help, send me the links to the sites you've found and I'll have a look." Taking a business card out of his wallet, he handed it to her. "My phone number and email address are on the back."

Her eyebrows rose when she read the card. "You're the chief executive of a biomedical company?"

"I started BioTech Industries ten years ago." From Katie's expression, he couldn't tell if she was impressed or puzzled by his career choice.

"What does your company do?"

"We're involved in a lot of different aspects of medicine and patient care. Our main focus is on creating high-tech devices that help people live normal lives."

Katie still seemed confused. "Mom said you're from New York City. Are you here on vacation?"

"Not for this visit. Someone from the tiny home village is using a new type of prosthetic my company's developing. I'm evaluating their results along with forty others and completing the trial report. After that, I'll contact potential investors to secure funding for phase two of the project."

"Is Richard the person who's on the trial?"

"He is. Have you met him?"

Katie smiled. "Sapphire Bay is a small town. We know almost everyone who lives here. His son comes to my after school program at The Welcome Center."

Diana picked up her coffee cup and took it across to the dishwasher. "In between making delicious meals for our guests and writing, Katie's helping a group of children create their own books."

"You're busy."

"I enjoy what I do." Katie glanced at the clock on the wall. "And talking about work, I need to prepare tonight's dinner. Otherwise, we'll have a lot of hungry guests wondering where their meals are."

Peter looked at the time. "I need to get back to work, too. Thanks for the coffee."

"You're welcome. I hope you're able to fund the next part of your project."

"So do I. The prosthetics are making a huge difference in people's lives." He picked up their coffee cups and took them across to the counter. "Remember to send me the self-publishing links you've found."

Katie bit her bottom lip. "Are you sure you have the time to help me?"

"I'll make the time." His softly spoken words brought another blush to Katie's cheeks. A warm protectiveness spread through his chest. The more he knew about her, the more special she seemed.

Katie opened a kitchen drawer and took out a pen and notebook. She scribbled something on a sheet of paper and handed it to him. "If you have any questions about what I send you, give me a call," she said quickly. "I'm available most afternoons."

Peter smiled. "Thanks. I'll remember." With a final farewell, he left the inn. He had no idea what was happening, but in some strange, unexpected way, Katie intrigued him. She was intelligent, sweet, and beautiful. And beneath her outgoing personality was a woman who was as unsure of her future as he was.

As HER DAD drove into the parking lot of The Kalispell Theatrical Company, Katie could hardly contain her excitement. Ever since Diana had told them she was having a Christmas-themed wedding, she'd dreamed about what their dresses would look like.

"Would you stop fidgeting," Penny said from beside her. "You're knocking my laptop."

Katie looked at the report her sister was reading. "I can't believe you're working. Aren't you excited about seeing the dresses?"

"I will be after I've worked out what the county wants me to do with the cottages on Anchor Lane," she muttered.

Mabel looked over her shoulder at Penny. "I thought they were happy for you to start renovating them."

"They are, but there's still a lot of red tape to go through. The Heritage Protection Society has some questions about the plans."

Allan frowned. "That doesn't sound great. Can they object to what's already been approved?"

"I don't think so. They looked at the plans a few weeks ago and didn't say anything."

"Don't let them worry you," their dad said. "I know the chairperson of the group. Percy Adams is a decent person. He wouldn't hold up the project if it's already gone through the planning and building departments."

Katie threw off her seatbelt and turned around. Diana and Barbara were pulling into the parking lot behind them.

Penny sighed and closed her laptop. "Anyone would think you're ten years old."

"I forgive your grumpiness, but you might want to plaster a fake smile on your face. Diana looks worried."

With an exaggerated smile, Penny glared at Katie. "Better?"

"Slightly."

Their mom picked up her bag. "Katie's right. Diana was a little pale this morning. Even if you don't like everything about the costumes, choose the one you like the best. We don't have time to look for anything else."

Katie jumped out of the truck and shivered. For someone

born and raised in Montana, she was still getting used to the crisp winter mornings. With a wave to Diana and Barbara, she quickly pulled up the zipper on her jacket and rushed to their vehicle.

As soon as Diana stepped out of the truck, Katie held her hands. "This is so exciting. I can't wait to see the costumes."

"I hope they're as good as we think they'll be."

"They will be." As soon as the rest of their family joined them, Katie asked, "Is everyone ready?"

Mabel grinned from beneath a fur-lined hat. "I've been ready for the last week. I can't wait to see what we look like."

A bubble of excitement made Katie grin. Neither could she.

CHAPTER 4

$\mathcal{M}$abel sighed. "Oh, my goodness. You're so handsome."

Katie peeked around the edge of the clothes rack and smiled. Her dad was standing in front of the full-length mirror, studying his reflection.

"I'm not sure about the vest. What do you think, Katie?"

She moved farther into the room. "I agree with Mom. You look great." The sparkly red vest looked perfect under the black jacket he'd chosen.

Katie didn't need to see her dad's relieved smile to know he'd been slightly worried.

"I'll send Ethan a photo," he said. "He might want to rent the same vests for him and Zac."

"That's a good idea." Mabel took a sparkly red dress off another rack. Holding the creation in front of her, she stood beside her husband. "We could be twins."

Allan kissed his wife's cheek. "The color suits you."

Diana touched Katie's arm. "Have you found anything?"

She was hoping her sister wouldn't ask. After her mom's

pep talk about choosing the best costume they found, Katie hadn't seen anything she liked.

Penny appeared from behind another rack. "I've found a dress for you." The gown she held toward her was incredible.

Katie didn't know what to say. The powder blue chiffon skirt was covered with silver snowflakes. When Penny turned it around, Katie couldn't resist touching the sweetheart neckline. It looked about the right size and it was definitely something she could wear to a Christmas-themed wedding. "It's beautiful. Are you sure it's available?"

"I checked with the costume coordinator before I took it off the rack. You should try it on."

Katie held the dress close to her chest and looked for the fitting rooms.

"They're over there," Diana said as she pointed to the far wall. "Barbara's trying on a dress, too."

Quickly, she hurried across the room. With everyone else happy with at least one option, she really wanted this dress to look good.

When she pulled back the heavy velvet curtain, Barbara turned from in front of the ornate mirror. The purple and blue floor-length dress she was wearing floated around her legs.

Barbara touched the skirt. "I was a little worried about finding something, but this is gorgeous."

"It's perfect." Katie loved the way the dress shimmered as her sister moved. "I can't imagine you wearing anything else."

"Neither can I. What about the dress you're holding? Are you trying it on?"

With an enthusiastic nod, Katie closed the curtain and took off her T-shirt and jeans. "I just hope it's okay. Mom, Dad, and Penny have already found something to wear."

"Think positive," Barbara said as she helped Katie lift the dress over her head. "I'll do up the zipper."

Katie held her breath as the dress slid down her body. So far, so good.

"You'd better breathe," Barbara said. "Otherwise, you'll turn as purple as my dress."

"It's all right for you," Katie moaned. "No one in our family has curves except me. If I find a dress that fits my bust, it's too big around my hips."

"Well, this one looks as though it'll fit you like a glove."

With a firm tug, Barbara pulled the zipper up the back of the dress. "Done! I told you it would fit."

Cautiously, Katie lifted her arms, then rolled her shoulders. "I can't believe how good it feels." As soon as she saw herself in the mirror, her mouth dropped open. "It's so pretty." The silver snowflakes looked even more dazzling under the fluorescent lights. And the bodice, with its sweetheart neckline and diamante beads, made the costume seem even more elegant.

Barbara tilted her head to the side. "Do you want to search for another dress or are you happy with this one?"

Katie grinned and picked up the wand that had fallen on the floor. With a flourish, she waved it in the air and tapped the top of her sister's head. "These two Cinderellas will definitely go to the ball."

Barbara laughed. "We're supposed to be Christmas bridesmaids, not Cinderellas."

With one last twirl in front of the mirror, Katie sighed. "We can be whoever we want to be. I hope Diana likes the dresses we've found."

"She will. Has she said anything about her dress?"

"Nothing. Has she told you about it?"

Barbara shook her head. "I'm hoping no news is good news. We'll never find a Christmas-themed bridal gown in the next two weeks."

Katie handed her sister the wand. "Who knows? With

three sisters and her parents helping her, anything's possible." And with a grin, she opened the curtain.

When her parents and sisters saw them, their collective sigh made Katie glad they'd come here today.

Now all they had to do was make sure the bride had a dress and everyone would be happy.

By Thursday, Peter was happy with the progress he'd made with his trial report. To clear his head before he analyzed the next series of tests, he was driving into town to speak to Pastor John.

The programs the local pastor was running were as good as any you'd find in a large city. But it was the man's drive and determination that Peter admired above everything else. If John thought a program or event could change a person's life, nothing stopped him from making that happen.

Today, regardless of what happened with the next phase of the trial, Peter wanted to make a difference, too.

Each time he visited Sapphire Bay, he'd noticed a growing number of young people and their parents living in the tiny home village. On his last visit, he'd spoken to John about what the families needed. With the community pitching in to provide household goods and groceries, their immediate needs were being met. It didn't take long to realize that having a good education and providing more employment opportunities would give the families a better life. And, hopefully, a more secure future than they had at the moment.

Parking his rental truck outside the church, Peter made his way into the reception area. Looking around the brightly decorated room, it was hard to imagine what this building must have been like before John arrived.

Andrea greeted him at the front counter. "Hi, Peter."

"Hi. I have an appointment with Pastor John. Is he still tutoring the hospitality class?"

"He is, but they should be finished soon. If you want to wait in the dining room, you're more than welcome."

"Thanks. I'll do that." With a grateful smile, he walked through a double set of doors. The dining room was sometimes used for hosting small events, but today it was almost empty. Sitting at a round table on the far side of the room was Shelley, John's wife.

"Have you been banished from your office?"

"Not quite," she replied. "I'm organizing some last-minute additions to the Christmas on Main Street events. It's easier to do it here."

An image of Katie's sparkling blue eyes filled his mind. "I spoke to Katie Terry the other day. She told me about some of the events."

"Did she ask if you want to help?"

Peter laughed. "She mentioned something about needing more Christmas elves. I'm fairly confident she won't have a six foot three costume available."

"You'd be surprised."

Another set of doors opened and a group of about twenty young people walked into the dining room.

"You'd better see John while you have the chance," Shelley said quickly. "Theo was here earlier wanting to interview him."

"Thanks."

"You're welcome. Don't let an elf costume stop you from coming to the events. People join us from all over Montana to be part of our Christmas program."

"Zac's already convinced me that I need to go."

"Good." She pointed behind him. "There's John."

The pastor of The Connect Church made his way across the room. "It's great to see you, Peter. Come on through to my office."

Shelley leaped out of her chair. "Can you sign this before you leave? We need a little more money for the Christmas baskets."

John's eyes gleamed. "Didn't you tell me the budget you'd set was more than enough?"

"And you said I'd need twice as much money. You were right." Shelley held a sheet of paper and a pen toward her husband. "Don't gloat. It isn't attractive."

John chuckled. "I don't often hear that I was right." He made an amendment to the document and handed it back to Shelley. "I've approved more money than what you think you'll need. Two more families are arriving at The Welcome Center this afternoon. They'll need Christmas gift baskets, too."

"Does Andrea and the rest of the team know?"

John nodded. "They're organizing their rooms now."

Shelley placed the sheet of paper on the table and smiled at Peter. "Enjoy your meeting with John. If he doesn't agree with what you suggest, come and see me. I have a secret weapon in the bottom drawer of my desk."

From the look in John's eyes, Peter didn't want to ask what it was.

Shelley's cheeks burned. "Ignore my husband. He has an overactive imagination."

"I don't know what you mean," John said with a grin. "Peter probably guessed that you're talking about my favorite candy."

He hadn't, but it was more appropriate than the other things he'd thought about.

With a sigh, Shelley turned to her husband. "You'd better speak to Peter before your next appointment arrives."

"Yes, ma'am."

Peter smiled when he saw the gleam in John's eyes. It was

easy to see how much in love they were. No matter how much he wanted it, finding someone who made him just as happy seemed like an impossibility.

After they were seated in John's office, Peter opened a folder. "I appreciate you talking to me. I know how crazy this time of the year is."

"It's the least I can do. Richard's made great progress since he was given the prosthetic leg. Thank you for taking a chance on him."

If it weren't for John and Zac's insistence that Richard was a good candidate, he wouldn't have made it into the trial. "If you'd called me a day later, we wouldn't have been able to accept his application. I'm glad we did, but that isn't why I'm here."

"I'm listening."

"My company has been looking at ways we can make a difference in communities. Last time I was here, I asked you what Sapphire Bay needs. I went through the list you sent me and I have a proposition for you." Peter handed John a sheet of paper. "BioTech would like to offer five students full college scholarships to Montana State University."

John's eyes widened. "That's an incredible offer."

"It's a start. I'm investigating some other initiatives we'd like to fund, but that will take a little more time."

John read the letter. "This will make an enormous difference to the students..."

Peter knew what had caused the stunned silence. The last paragraph of the letter contained an amount of money that was more than the church had raised all year.

John looked up and frowned. "Is this for real?"

"It's as real as it gets. Providing someone with a new limb helps them physically. What you're doing in the church and in The Welcome Center gives people hope. As well as the scholarships, I'd like BioTech to support the programs you're running."

Tears shone from John's eyes. "All I can say is thank you. It's a constant struggle to fund what we're doing."

Peter knew just how difficult it had been. "I spoke to Shelley a couple of months ago. The donation will make it easier to plan ahead." He looked at the sheet of paper. "I only have one condition. I don't want anyone to know I funded any of this."

John looked genuinely confused. "Why?"

An uncomfortable tightness filled Peter's chest. "People look at you differently when they know how much money you have. I want to be treated like everyone else."

With a thoughtful nod, John agreed to his request. "I'll tell everyone the money came from an anonymous donor. If you ever want to talk about what happened, I'm a good listener."

Peter sighed. "Thanks, but it was a long time ago."

"Time doesn't make any difference to how we feel."

Taking an envelope out of his pocket, Peter handed it to John. "No, but this will."

John's hand shook when he accepted the check.

"My staff will liaise with the university to work out the best way of paying for the scholarships. I'll leave it up to you and Shelley to finalize the details and choose the recipients."

Peter smiled as he stood. John wasn't often lost for words, but he still looked shocked by the donation. "If you have any questions, you can either ask me or call the head of our finance team. Her details are on the bottom of the letter."

John opened his arms and hugged Peter. "This means more than you can imagine. Thank you."

"You're welcome. I'm looking forward to seeing what you do with the money." And with a final hug, Peter left John to think about what had just happened.

✳

KATIE SAT beside Nora and read the ten-year-old's story. "This is wonderful. I like the way Marley can jump as high as a horse. He must be a very special dog."

"Dogs can't jump as high as horses," Charlie, Nora's friend, said from the other side of the table. "Even dogs with long legs couldn't do that."

"Marley can," Nora said with certainty. "He's eaten some magic beans that make him extra strong."

Katie watched excitement build on Charlie's face. He loved anything to do with magic. "Where did he get the beans?"

Nora tapped her pencil against her chin. "I haven't decided yet. He could have found them in the vegetable garden or someone could have given them to him."

Adele, the youngest budding author in their writing group, leaped out of her chair. "I know. Santa could have given him the beans."

From Nora's smile, Katie guessed she liked Adele's idea.

"Can I add another page into my story?" Nora asked Katie.

"Of course, you can. Do you know where you'd like to put it?"

She turned to the second page. "It could go here. And Santa could ask Marley to help him deliver the Christmas presents."

"What else can Marley do with the beans?" Charlie asked.

While Nora told him about Marley's magical abilities, Katie moved around the table. For the last two months, she'd met a group of children at The Welcome Center. Each Thursday they'd worked on their stories, polishing the text and drawing pictures for their very own books.

Andy, one of the older students, had written a story about

a twelve-year-old's rocket mission to Mars. Katie had enjoyed it so much she'd encouraged him to enter it into a writing competition.

She laughed at something he said and carried on to her next student.

"Hi, Mr. Bennett," Nora yelled across the room. "Come and see what we're doing."

Katie looked up and saw Peter standing uncertainly in the doorway. "It's okay. You're welcome to join us."

"We're making our own books," Nora said proudly.

"That sounds exciting."

Aware that Peter's gaze was focused on her, Katie's heart pounded. "This is our final week to edit the text," she said. "Next week, we'll finish the drawings."

Adele hurried around the table. "And then we can show our families." She handed him her work book. "This is my story. It's about a baby mouse called Mindy. She's white and cuddly and loves eating chocolate."

"She sounds like a very happy mouse."

Katie's heart melted as Adele told Peter all about Mindy.

He listened carefully to what she said, asking questions that made the six-year-old smile. His kindness and gentleness made Katie sigh.

Andy looked at the clock on the wall. "It's almost time to leave."

Charlie groaned. "But I want to know what happens to Nora's magic dog."

"You can ask her while we're having a cookie," his brother replied. "Mom doesn't want to be late home."

"Andy's right," Katie said. "Talk to Nora in the dining room. Remember to bring your drawings with you next Thursday."

"I will," Adele yelled from across the room.

With a flurry of activity, everyone packed their bags and hurried out of the meeting room.

Peter's eyes widened. "I've never seen children move so quickly."

Katie lifted her hand and beckoned him toward the doorway. When he was standing beside her, she smiled. "This is why they were in such a hurry."

The children were standing in front of a table, selecting cookies from a plate.

"Nora's Aunt Megan owns Sweet Treats. She bakes fresh cookies and brings them to the center before she picks up Nora. I don't know whether it's creating a book or the cookies that everyone enjoys more."

"I'd say it's their books. Look at the two children over there."

While eating their cookies, Nora and Charlie leaned together, talking excitedly.

Katie thought the children would enjoy creating stories, but she hadn't anticipated the other benefits. "This class has been good for all of them. Charlie and Andy were shy when they joined the group. Once they got to know everyone, they were much more relaxed. And Nora and Adele have learned to be a little more patient and listen to other people's ideas. We usually have two more children with us, but Jack and Amelia couldn't make today's class."

"When did you start the group?"

"A couple of months ago. As soon as Mom told Pastor John I'm a writer, he asked if I'd organize a children's writing club. I didn't mind and it hasn't taken a lot of time."

"I'm impressed. It can't be easy working at the inn, writing, and doing this."

Katie blushed. "It's not a big deal."

"It is to the children."

She guessed it was. They were all looking forward to seeing their finished stories. And they'd be even more excited when they saw the Christmas surprise she'd organized for them.

Katie turned to face Peter. "I haven't seen you at The Welcome Center before."

"I've come a few times. John and his volunteers are doing things you don't see very often."

"We need these types of centers in Los Angeles. The homeless shelters can only do so much to help people." She watched the children enjoy each other's company. "Places like this give everyone a sense of purpose."

"What does it give you?"

Instead of replying quickly, she thought about what she'd learned. "Volunteering at the center makes me appreciate how important family is. For the last few years, I've taken that for granted."

"Everyone likes to feel connected to someone," Peter said softly.

His blue eyes were watching the children, but she suspected his thoughts were a million miles away. "Will you see your family at Christmas?"

Peter shook his head. "My parents and sister are having Christmas with my aunt in Montreal. They won't be home until mid-January."

"That's a shame. They could have enjoyed the Christmas events in Sapphire Bay."

"They would have liked them. Although I might have had to keep Mom away from The Christmas Tree Farm. You weren't joking when you said they have some amazing gifts."

"It's one of our hidden gems." Katie waved at Adele's mom as she arrived to collect her daughter. "And talking about gems, I'd better tidy the meeting room. Someone else is using it tonight."

"Do you need a hand?"

"It's okay. I only have to push the tables to the side of the room and stack the chairs. Have you finished your report?"

"Not yet, but I'm getting there." Peter cleared his throat. "I was wondering if you'd like to meet for coffee tomorrow? I read the information you sent me about self-publishing and I have a few questions."

Katie wasn't sure why Peter looked so nervous, but it was cute. "I'd like that. Does two-thirty suit you? We could meet at the café in The Fairy Forest."

Peter's eyes widened. "The Fairy Forest?"

"I'll send you the address."

"Is this another one of your hidden gems?"

Katie grinned. "How did you guess?" Impulsively, she hugged Peter. "I hope you feel connected to Sapphire Bay." As soon as his body tensed, she knew she'd made a mistake. She liked Peter. He was kind, thoughtful, and had a great job, but that didn't mean he felt the same way about her. And even if he did, it wouldn't make any difference. She was going back to Los Angeles in a few months.

Dropping her arms, she quickly stepped away, hoping he didn't notice the blush heating her face. "Oops. Sorry." And before he could reply, she hurried back to the meeting room.

With another volunteer looking after the children in the dining room, she should be relieved that everything went so well this afternoon. But hugging Peter wasn't the most intelligent thing she'd ever done.

She just hoped he still wanted to meet for coffee with a woman who had more on her mind than was good for her.

CHAPTER 5

*D*iana opened the dishwasher and placed her breakfast bowl inside. "You really need to stop hugging people you've only just met."

Katie's sisters had repeated the same thing so many times that she was beginning to think there was something wrong with her. "He didn't seem to mind, but I'm worried he won't want to meet me for coffee."

"What did he say after you hugged him?"

"I don't know," Katie said miserably. "I left so quickly that I barely looked at him."

"Have you talked to him at all since yesterday afternoon?"

"No." Katie bit her bottom lip. "I could call him? At least that way I'll know if he thinks I'm crazy."

"You aren't crazy. You're an extrovert."

That didn't make her feel any better. She really was trying to be less enthusiastic, but it wasn't easy. With a sigh, she added another cup of flour to the mixing bowl in front of her. Baking was so much better than worrying about what she'd done yesterday. Especially when she was baking her favorite muffins. "If Peter doesn't arrive at the café, I'll speak to Daniella about your wedding."

"Do you have a copy of our spreadsheet?"

"It's on my laptop. What's happening with your gown?"

A smile lit Diana's face. "I didn't buy the dress I thought I would."

"And that makes you happy?"

Her sister shook her head. "The surprise you'll get when you see it will make me happy."

"Does that mean you aren't showing anybody your dress before you get married?"

Barbara walked into the kitchen. "I asked her the same question last night. My guess is that Diana's wearing an elf costume."

"I'll be wearing one of those at the Christmas parade, but not on my wedding day."

Taking a large spoon out of a drawer, Katie divided the muffin batter into the paper liners. "You didn't bring anything home with you from Kalispell, so I'm guessing you found something on the Internet. I hope you've remembered what happened to Penny."

Diana took a banana out of the fruit bowl. "I didn't buy it off the Internet, either. If anyone's looking for me, I'm taking the Williamsons to Bigfork."

Katie looked through the kitchen window. "Don't be too late coming home. It looks as though a storm's on the way."

"I'll be careful. Good luck with your date."

Barbara turned a wide-eyed stare toward Katie. "You're going on a date?"

"Don't get too excited. I might have scared Peter off."

"How?"

"She hugged him," Diana said as she left the room.

"I didn't mean to, but it burst out of me." Katie carried the muffin tins across to the oven. It was better than seeing the frown on Barbara's face.

"Did he seem upset?"

"I didn't stay around long enough to find out."

Barbara poured some cereal into a bowl. "If he turns up for your date, you'll know he didn't mind."

That was true, but it wasn't what was worrying her the most. Feeling anything other than friendship toward him was a complication she didn't need.

PETER STOOD in the entryway of The Fairy Forest. For the tenth time, he checked his watch. There was still another few minutes until Katie was due to meet him. Whether she turned up was an entirely different story.

Yesterday, she'd left the dining room so quickly he didn't know what he'd done to offend her. In hindsight, he could have said something to make her feel less embarrassed about hugging him. But that would have assumed he was able to string two words together—which he wasn't.

With Katie's arms wrapped around him, he'd imagined what it would be like to be close to her all the time. But those thoughts were dangerous and would only lead to heartache. She had a life away from Sapphire Bay, just like he did. Within the next few months, they'd both leave the small Montana town and return to their normal lives.

Even so, he hated to think that being around him would make her feel uncomfortable. From the first day he'd met Katie, he knew she liked hugging people. Even people who didn't like touching anyone couldn't be offended by the good-natured way she expressed herself.

"Hello. Can I help you?"

Peter looked over his shoulder. The young woman who'd

spoken to him was dressed like a fairy. Her bright red dress and gold wings sparkled under the fluorescent lights. "I'm okay. I'm waiting for a friend."

"That's all right. If you'd like any information about The Fairy Forest, I'll be in the main events room." She pointed at a door shaped like an oversized tree trunk. "It's through there."

"No one's ever told me to walk through a tree to get into another room."

"You probably don't meet too many fairies and goblins, either. I'm Daniella. I own The Fairy Forest."

Peter shook the hand she held out. "It's nice to meet you."

The door to the outside world opened and Katie stepped into the entryway. With her red hair hidden beneath a fluffy orange hat and a purple ski jacket wrapped around her body, she looked like she was ready to hit the ski slopes. For a split second, her gaze focused on him before moving to his right. A knot tightened in his chest, reminding him that what she felt about him shouldn't matter so much.

"Hi, Daniella."

"Welcome back. I was just thinking about you."

Katie's eyes widened. "You were?"

"One of my suppliers sent me their latest catalog. They have some amazing 'Just Married' lights that would look lovely at Diana and Ethan's reception. They could be a surprise for when they arrive."

"That's a fabulous idea. Can I look at the catalog after I've been to the café with Peter?"

"Sounds great." Daniella smiled at Peter. "If you want to impress Katie, buy her a hot chocolate with cinnamon sprinkles. It's her favorite drink."

Katie grinned. "And if you include a Christmas cookie, I'll be your friend for life."

The knot in his chest unwound. If all it took was a cookie,

he'd buy her a lifetime's supply. "You can order as many as you like."

She stepped toward him, then stopped. With a barely audible groan, she motioned toward a doorway surrounded by giant flowers. "If you're ready to go into the café, it's this way."

He looked into Katie's troubled eyes and sighed. He'd never been more ready for anything.

KATIE STEPPED into the café and tried not to focus on her almost touching moment with Peter. Before she left the inn, she'd decided to keep her hands in her pockets. That way, she wouldn't touch him and make him feel uncomfortable. But, she was so focused on what she'd decided to do, she hadn't seen him when she walked into The Fairy Forest.

One moment's inattention and she was nearly back to where she'd been yesterday. Luckily, this was her favorite place in town. She couldn't worry about much when she was sipping a delicious mug of hot chocolate and listening to Christmas carols.

Taking a deep breath, she let the magic of The Fairy Forest Café wash over her. Daniella had poured her heart and soul into creating a whimsical, magical environment for people to enjoy, and she'd succeeded. Sunlight poured through the double-height windows and most of the tables were crowded with adults and children. Even when she was feeling a little down, the bright rainbow of flowers painted on the walls lifted her spirits.

Peter seemed surprised when he saw the green, leaf-shaped tables and the buttercup light fittings. "Apart from when I visited Disneyland, I've never seen anything like this."

"It's amazing, isn't it? Daniella has a friend who builds

props for movie sets. Most of the furniture and decorations came from him, but some of the furniture was made locally. We bring all our guests here."

"I bet they enjoy it."

"They do. If they have children, it can be the highlight of their visit, especially if they go to one of the fairy events." She smiled at the waitress who took them across to a table. Dressed in a purple fairy costume, her wings fluttered with each step she took.

Peter leaned toward Katie and whispered, "I feel slightly under-dressed."

"Don't worry. You aren't the only one who isn't dressed as a fairy or a goblin. There are at least ten Muggles in the room, if you don't count the pirates."

"It's just as well I've read the Harry Potter books. Otherwise, I wouldn't know you're talking about people with non-magical abilities."

A bubble of pleasure skipped along her spine. "Do you realize how perfect you are? Not only are you kind, intelligent, and handsome, but you read children's books." When she saw Peter's surprised expression, she groaned. "I've done it again, haven't I?"

Instead of being embarrassed, he laughed. "You can tell me those things as often as you like. But, if my ego gets too big, I'll tell everyone it's your fault."

Before she could reply, the waitress stopped at a table. Katie quickly sat down. So much for being careful about what she did and said around Peter. If her sisters could see her, they'd be laughing by now.

After they'd placed their order, Katie cleared her throat. "As well as apologizing for what I said, I'm sorry for hugging you yesterday."

Peter's eyebrows rose. "You don't need to apologize."

"Yes, I do. Sometimes I get overexcited and do things I shouldn't."

"And hugging is one of those things?"

Sadly, Katie nodded. "A lot of people don't like being touched by someone they don't know. I try really hard to keep a few feet away from people, but it isn't easy."

"You don't need to worry about me. I'm okay with being hugged."

Katie breathed a sigh of relief. "I was worried I'd spoiled our new friendship."

"It would take a lot more than a hug to make me think any less of you. Besides, you aren't the only person in Sapphire Bay who likes hugging people. I was walking along Main Street last week and a woman was giving people hugs as a fundraiser for a Christmas program."

"That sounds like the perfect job for me."

Peter laughed. "It could be, if you didn't want to be a writer. Which brings me to one of the reasons we're here." He opened the laptop he'd brought with him and turned it around. "I read the information you sent through about self-publishing. It sounded reasonably straightforward, so I downloaded some formatting software and tried it. This is how a report I wrote came out as an e-book."

Katie studied the text. "Can I turn to the next page?"

"Of course, you can. Use the mousepad in front of the keys."

While she was studying the text, Peter sat silently across the table.

Everything inside the document looked professional. From the headings to the scene breaks, no one would guess the e-book wasn't produced by a publishing house.

"How long did it take to format the report?" she asked.

"It only took a few seconds. I had to do a couple of adjustments afterward but, once you know how the software works, it isn't difficult."

Katie slid the laptop back to Peter. "It looks great."

The waitress arrived with their order.

With two cups of hot chocolate and a plate of cookies between them, Katie couldn't have been happier. "This looks lovely," she said to the waitress. "Thank you."

"You're welcome. We baked the cookies this morning. They're delicious." With a friendly smile, she left to help another group of customers.

Peter watched the new arrivals find a table. "For a small town, the café's busy."

"It's usually like this, especially after school." Katie picked up a spoon and dipped it into the creamy froth on the top of her drink. Last night, after everyone had gone to bed, she'd thought long and hard about what she wanted to do with the books she'd written. Seeing Peter's e-book made her feel even more certain she was doing the right thing.

"I called my agent this morning. I've decided to self-publish my stories."

"Congratulations. What made you change your mind?"

"I've been thinking about it for a long time. A friend who's self-published offered to show me how to load the files onto each retail platform. They even gave me the name of a graphic designer who can make new covers for me."

"It sounds as though you've got everything organized."

"There's still a lot of things I don't know, but I'm tired of waiting for the publishing houses to decide if they'll buy my books."

"You're taking control of your career."

Katie nodded. "I guess I am." Instead of second-guessing herself, she was proud of her decision—even if it was the complete opposite of what she'd wanted to do.

"I could format your books if that helps."

"You're busy with your own work. If you tell me which software you used, I should be able to work it out."

"I don't mind helping."

"What about your report?"

"It won't make a difference to my schedule. Besides, the sooner your books are formatted, the quicker you can sell them."

Katie knew it wasn't that easy. "From what my friend told me, there are all kinds of things I'll need to do to help people find my books." She pulled a piece of paper from her pocket and looked at the list she'd made. "I already have a website and a Facebook and Instagram account. I like my book covers, but I need to see if they appeal to children. Once my books are published, I'll start marketing them. There are so many promotion sites that I don't know where to start."

Peter picked up a cookie. "Doesn't one of your sisters work in social media?"

"Barbara does, but I don't want to bother her. She's already spent a lot of time helping me."

Peter grinned and, not for the first time, Katie's heart pounded. He had such a genuine, happy smile that it made people smile back at him.

"It's just as well you've met me, then."

"Don't tell me. As well as being the chief executive of a successful company, you're a marketing genius?"

"I'm hopeless when it comes to marketing, but I employ a team of people who are very good. Would you like me to ask them if they have any recommendations?"

"I'm not sure they'll know about book advertising sites, but it wouldn't hurt to ask."

"Even if they've never marketed children's books, they know about buyer behavior and what makes people look at different ads. Sometimes, that's all you need to start a revolution."

Katie grinned. "I don't want to start a revolution. All I want is for someone to buy my books and love them as much as I do."

"If your stories are as amazing as you are, they'll fly off the digital shelves."

The heat of a blush swept across her face. If Peter said things like that, she'd get the wrong idea about why they were here. "Thanks for the vote of confidence, but I still have a long way to go before I can sell anything."

And even though Peter had offered to help, she was still worried. In all her plans, she'd ignored the one obvious problem.

What if no one liked her books?

CHAPTER 6

The following afternoon, Peter sat at his desk, studying the latest trial results. They were even better than the data he'd already included in his report.

After three years of pushing his staff to think beyond what they'd ever imagined a prosthetic limb could become, he was almost ready to start phase two of the project. He just hoped the funders he'd contacted were still interested in supporting the project.

His cell phone pinged and he opened the message from David O'Dowd, the Clinical Director of BioTech. When he read the brief email, his heart sank.

Throughout the entire project every scrap of information was classified as top secret. Until they were ready to commercially manufacture the prosthetic limbs, his company couldn't afford to let anyone know what they were doing.

With his heart pounding, he called David. "How did it happen?"

"I don't know, but we're working on it. The only good thing is that the person who leaked the report doesn't have the latest information."

Peter opened the link David had included in his email. At least the story hadn't made the front page of *The New York Times*. "What did our legal team say?"

"They want us to launch an investigation into how the data was released. Solomon's already onto it. They're also fielding questions from other companies as well as the public."

"Have you contacted the trial participants?"

"Janice is doing that as we speak. We're reassuring them that their personal information hasn't been compromised and reminding them not to speak to the media. You'll probably get a few phone calls."

Peter rubbed his forehead. Receiving a few phone calls was the least of his worries. Releasing any trial outcomes before the final data had been analyzed could jeopardize their funding. "I'll call Matt and Antonia. They'll want to let their staff know what's happened."

"Already done. After the forensic team has finished in our offices, they'll head across to Antonia and Matt's staff and look at their computers. Everyone who has a work laptop is bringing it into the office tonight. It won't take long to work out how the leak happened."

He hoped not. Any breach in security was taken extremely seriously, especially when multimillion-dollar deals were involved. "Give me a few minutes to read the information you've sent through. I'll call you as soon as I've finished."

"Try not to worry. It could have been a lot worse."

Peter looked at the half-finished report sitting on his desk. If anyone got their hands on that information, three years of intensive research would be down the drain. "If you need to call me, use my personal cell phone number."

"Good idea. I'll talk to you soon."

After checking his voicemail, Peter turned off his work

cell phone. The only other time he'd done that was when his dad had a heart attack. He'd wanted to focus on his family and not be tempted to answer any calls about the company's latest projects.

This time, the only thing he wanted to do was find the person responsible for leaking the information. He only hoped that if they'd known how important the information was, they wouldn't have done it.

"I THOUGHT you'd finished work for the day."

Peter looked up from his laptop at Zac. "We had an emergency."

"Is everything okay?"

"We're still working on it. How's Tiffany?"

"Awake and ready for the Santa Parade. Are you still coming?"

After three hours of focusing on more work issues, the last thing he wanted to do was stand outside in the cold, watching a line of Christmas floats. But he'd promised Katie he'd be there. "When are you leaving?"

"In about ten minutes. I just have to find my reindeer antlers and then we're off."

Despite being stressed about what was happening in New York, Peter smiled. "Is that a small-town tradition you haven't told me about?"

"I don't know if it's a tradition, but Willow's on the Christmas Festival Committee. They're encouraging everyone to dress up in some kind of Christmas-themed costume. Don't worry. I have the perfect accessory for you."

"I'm not a local, so the directive doesn't include me."

Zac laughed. "Nice try, but you've been here so often you're part of the community. I'll see you at the front door in ten minutes." And with another chuckle, he left the office.

Peter checked his watch. He had just enough time to call David before he discovered what surprise costume Zac had in mind for him. As long as it wasn't an elf costume, he was happy to wear it.

With more care than usual, he locked the laptop and the papers he was reading in a drawer and called his clinical director. Now, more than ever, they needed to be super vigilant about security. If anyone saw the startling results his team had recorded, they'd want more than information about the prosthetics.

They'd break every rule known to mankind to get their hands on the formula they'd used to produce the neural gel. Because that, above everything else, had implications that went far beyond the prosthetic limbs.

KATIE ADJUSTED her elf hat and smiled at her dad.

With the camera on his cell phone ready, he snapped a photo of her with Barbara, Penny, and their excited dog.

"One more for good luck," their mom said as she rushed forward to straighten the ruffle at Penny's neck. "I'll post the photos on Facebook."

Penny groaned. "Do you have to?"

"It's a human-interest story," Mabel said as she fluffed Barbara's angel wings. "You haven't looked this cute since you were seven years old."

"Is that supposed to make us feel better or worse about Dad taking the photos?"

"Better, of course."

Katie glanced down Main Street, hoping to divert their mom's attention before she noticed Charlie had eaten the decoration off the bottom of Barbara's costume. "Diana's coming. We should wait for her."

Allan waved to his daughter. "I wonder how her meeting went with Pastor John."

"Hopefully, there aren't any problems with having her wedding at the church." Mabel beckoned Diana forward. "Come and have your photo taken with your sisters."

Charlie gave a happy woof and sat obediently at Diana's feet. If you didn't know what he'd been up to, you'd think he was the best-behaved dog in the world.

Wearing an exact copy of Katie's candy-striped elf costume, Diana stood beside Penny. "I saw Megan and William on the way here. The floats are leaving from outside the library in ten minutes."

Mabel consulted her watch. "That gives us just enough time to take some more photos, then find a good place to watch the parade. You can tell me where Wyatt, Ethan, and Theo have gone after we've finished."

Katie looked at her sisters and grinned. She knew exactly where they were and so would their parents after the Santa parade traveled past them.

BY THE TIME Peter arrived in town with Zac and his family, hundreds of people were lining the sidewalk on either side of Main Street. With fairy lights glowing from the Christmas trees outside each store and the colorful costumes people were wearing, it definitely felt like Christmas was just around the corner.

Zac pushed Tiffany's stroller ahead of them, leading them through the crowd. When Willow had told Peter about the number of people coming to town for the Santa parade, he hadn't believed her. It wasn't as if the small Montana town was close to a lot of bigger cities. But for reasons that probably had a lot to do with nostalgia, Main Street was buzzing with people of all ages.

Pushing his elf hat out of his eyes, he touched his ears. Zac had called it fate when he'd found the large, plastic ears in a party planning store in Polson. Peter called it bad luck. But maybe it was an omen. If the technologically advanced prosthetics his company was making flopped, he could always design 3D limbs for all kinds of fantasy creatures.

"Don't wiggle them too much," Willow said. "They might fall off."

"Zac used an entire tube of body paste to stick them in place. They aren't going anywhere."

"Will you be able to take them off before you go to bed?"

"I hope so." With a senior board meeting tomorrow morning, the large, pointy ears needed to be gone before anyone else saw them.

He smiled at a woman dressed as Mrs. Claus. It was just as well most of the people walking along Main Street were wearing some kind of Christmas decoration or costume. At least he didn't stand out like a sore thumb.

Looking above the heads of the people in front of him, he saw the town's Christmas tree. Decorated in bright lights and glittering, super-sized decorations, it was even more impressive than it was during the day.

Zac waited for them before pointing to a gap in the crowd. "We should stand here for the parade. It doesn't look as though we'll get a better view from anywhere else."

Before another person stood in front of them, they moved closer to the road. As far as Peter was concerned, they couldn't have chosen a better spot. Behind them, Sweet Treats was full of customers, all looking for the perfect Christmas candy.

Willow tapped someone on the shoulder and Barbara

Terry turned around. It didn't surprise Peter that he hadn't recognized her. With a white angel costume keeping her warm, and her face partially covered by a fur-trimmed hat, she could have stepped out of the page of a fashion magazine. He glanced at the rest of her family, searching for Katie, but she wasn't there.

Mabel sent him a friendly wave before moving toward him. "I like your hat and ears. What do you think of our Christmas events?"

Peter had seen the Facebook posts and newspaper articles about what was happening in Sapphire Bay in December. Even compared to New York City, it was a huge achievement. "This is the first event I've been to and, so far, I'm impressed. I was working when the town turned on the Christmas lights for the first time."

"That's a shame. We sang Christmas carols, roasted marshmallows, and gave everyone a cup of eggnog. But don't worry, there's plenty more for you to see and do. Tomorrow night, Pastor John's hosting the annual carol competition in the church. It starts at seven o'clock."

Zac lifted Tiffany out of her stroller. "As well as the carols, Mabel's organized a gingerbread house competition. Coming in the top ten is a fiercely contested achievement."

Peter's eyes widened. "You entered?"

"Of course, I did," Zac said without cracking a smile. "Some of the Christmas scenes from last year were amazing."

"I took my entry into town this morning," Willow added. "It doesn't cost anything to listen to the carols or enter the competition, but we leave a bucket at the door for donations. All the money goes toward the Christmas Wish Program."

Mabel held her hand to her ear. "That sounds like the high school band. The parade must have started." After straightening the halo on her head, she stroked Tiffany's hand. "It only seems like yesterday that my girls were this age. Time goes by so fast."

Peter had thought the same thing when he saw Tiffany. On his previous trip to Sapphire Bay, she was only four months old. In the last month she'd become more aware of what was going on around her. Her chubby cheeks often broke into smiles and her giggles filled the house with sunshine.

Thinking of sunshine reminded him of Katie. His gaze searched the crowded street, but he couldn't see her.

Mabel smiled. "If you're looking for Katie, she'll be here in a few minutes."

Peter hoped she arrived before the band walked past. For the last few days, all she'd talked about was the Santa parade. For her, it was a trip down memory lane, a chance to recapture some of the Christmas spirit that had disappeared when her grandma died, and an opportunity to reconnect with her family and friends.

And maybe, if he was lucky, tonight's parade would create new memories that included him.

CHAPTER 7

*K*atie couldn't believe how well her two brothers-in-law and future brother-in-law were doing in the parade. It had taken more than a little arm-twisting to get Ethan, Wyatt, and Theo to dress as elves but, somehow, she'd managed to do it. In his defense, Theo probably had the best excuse not to be here. As a journalist and the only radio DJ in town, he felt a moral obligation to report on the news and not be part of it.

When she pointed out that being here tonight would give him first-hand experience of being a Christmas elf *and* unlimited access to Santa, his horror had turned to resignation.

In hindsight, showing everyone the elf costumes before the parade wasn't a good idea. Her sisters thought the red-and-white striped stockings and cute green tunics would look adorable on their dearly beloveds. It was unfortunate the men in their lives didn't share their enthusiasm.

Without a little bribery leading up to tonight, she doubted she would have had enough elves to hand out the candy.

As they waved and smiled at the people lining the sidewalk, Wyatt hurried back to the elf float. With more enthusiasm than he'd shown all night, he refilled his candy bucket. "You didn't tell me this would be so much fun."

Katie had to stop herself from saying, "I told you so." Wyatt had been particularly vocal in his refusal to wear the elf costume. "You can thank me later," she said as she refilled her own bucket.

Theo grabbed her hand and pulled her toward the sidewalk. "Quick. Your dad wants a photo of us." Before she knew what was happening, Ethan and Wyatt stood beside them, all grinning into the lens of her dad's cell phone.

Her mom was busy taking her own photos. It wasn't often you could surprise her, but seeing her sons-in-law standing in elf costumes seemed to make her extremely happy.

Katie smiled at her dad, then looked at the next group of people. Her heart gave a nervous flutter when she saw Peter standing with Willow and Zac.

Reaching into her bucket, she handed him a candy cane. "I like your elf hat and ears," she yelled over the din of the band.

"Thanks. They were Zac's idea."

"Do you want to help us give away candy?"

Peter held his hand to his ear. "I can't hear you."

Judging by his mischievous grin, she could almost guarantee he'd heard her. Instead of repeating herself, she held onto his jacket and pulled him forward. "Santa will be forever grateful for your help. Just be careful around the float and only give one piece of candy to each person."

"I'm not dressed like an elf."

She reached up and touched his ears. "You look perfect." The gleam in his eyes tempted her to do something she would regret. So, instead of kissing his smiling lips, she handed him her candy bucket. "Good luck."

Hurrying back to the float, she picked up another bucket

and walked back to Peter. When she'd told him about the Santa parade, he had no idea she had an ulterior motive. But with Zac's help, she'd managed to get him involved in one of the most enjoyable events in town.

Long after he returned to New York City, she hoped he remembered tonight with fondness. Because, regardless of how weird it felt to become an honorary elf, he would make a lot of children's dreams come true.

By the end of the night, the temperature had taken a serious nose-dive, leaving everyone who'd helped dismantle the elf float feeling like Popsicles. Even rushing around the Christmas market wasn't enough to warm everyone's hands and feet.

If it weren't for Pastor John inviting them to the church for something to eat and drink, they would have filled a café to overflowing.

"I can't believe we handed out so much candy," Peter said as he sat beside Katie. "There must have been more than two thousand people at the parade."

"Santa's Secret Helpers outdid themselves," Pastor John said proudly as he joined them.

Katie sipped her hot chocolate. "In more ways than one. I've seen the number of Christmas gift baskets waiting to be delivered. It must have taken a long time to organize them."

"It did, but the community was extremely generous." Pastor John helped himself to a cookie. "The publicity we received from last year's program helped motivate everyone. They could see the difference the gift baskets made in people's lives."

Peter frowned. "I've never heard of Santa's Secret Helpers."

"They're a group of volunteers who organize all the Christmas events in Sapphire Bay," Katie replied, "including the Christmas Wish Program and the gift baskets the church delivers. They do an amazing job."

"An amazing *secret* job," Pastor John told Peter. "Only a handful of people know who the helpers are."

"Can I assume you and Katie are part of Santa's Secret Helpers?" Peter asked.

Pastor John held his finger to his lips. "You can, but don't say anything to anyone."

Katie watched Peter's surprised expression. "It must sound like we're overreacting, but Sapphire Bay is so small that it's hard to keep anything a secret. I only joined last month when Emma told me about it. She owns a marketing and advertising business based in town." She looked around the room and pointed to a woman with long blond hair. "That's Kylie. She's one of the founding members, along with Bailey, who works with Zac at the medical clinic. Mom has helped with some of the programs and my sisters and Shelley, John's wife, help, too."

Pastor John sipped his mug of coffee. "We're always looking for people to help run the programs. You wouldn't be interested, would you?"

Peter didn't think it was fair to volunteer when he was going home in January. "I'm not sure how much help I'll be. I need to finish the report I'm writing as soon as possible. By the time that's done, Christmas will be almost over. A few weeks later, I'll be living in New York."

"You could help me deliver some of the Christmas gift baskets," Katie said. "We have more than fifty to take to homes where finances are a little tight."

"If that's too much, you could help with the Christmas wishes." Pastor John handed him the plate of cookies. "Even though it's called the Christmas Wish Program, we help people throughout the year."

"What types of wishes do you make come true?"

"We consider almost anything. We've bought wheelchairs, new bicycles, an electric scooter, and work clothes for people starting their first job," John said.

"Don't forget the cell phone and the family day out on the steamboat in Polson," Katie added. "It's amazing to see a person's reaction when we give them their wishes."

Peter felt the same way when he saw people use his company's prosthetic limbs. "It sounds like something I'd like to be part of. How do you fund the wishes?"

"We beg and borrow from any business that will listen." John stopped talking and frowned. "Don't even think about it."

"If it—"

John glanced at Katie, then back at Peter. "Delivering the gift boxes will be more than enough." His cell phone beeped and he looked at the message. "I'm needed at the tiny home village. If you see Shelley, let her know where I've gone. I'll give her a call as soon as I can."

His wife chose that moment to walk into the dining room. She handed John a ski jacket and hat. "Ethan was sent the same text. Be careful. It's started to snow."

"I'll be back as soon as I can." Leaving a quick kiss on Shelley's lips, John hurried out of the room, followed closely by Ethan.

"I hope it isn't anything too serious," Peter said softly.

Shelley sighed. "Christmas is a stressful time. John has more callouts in December than in any other month."

"Is he the only pastor in Sapphire Bay?"

"He is. Luckily, Zac, Ethan, and Bailey have set up a roster to assist with any mental health emergencies. Before they arrived, it was even worse." Shelley smiled at the half-eaten plate of cookies. "If you'd like something hot to eat, there's apple pie in the kitchen."

Katie grinned. "That sounds yummy."

"In that case, follow me."

As they got up and walked toward the kitchen, Peter looked at the men and women who'd volunteered tonight. They'd made Christmas extra special for a lot of people. If they could decorate the floats and wear tinsel-covered costumes, he could do more to help the community, too.

When they were in the kitchen, he took the pie Shelley gave him. "Thanks. It smells delicious."

"It's my mom's favorite recipe."

Katie sighed as she took her first bite. "It tastes fantastic. We can give you a hand to take the other pies out to everyone."

"That would be great, but finish your dessert first."

As Shelley took a stack of plates out of the cupboard, Peter thought about how he could support what Santa's Secret Helpers was doing. "Do either of you know if there are any Christmas wishes you haven't been able to do because of the cost?"

Katie pointed her spoon toward Shelley. "You're talking to the right person. Shelley's an accountant. As well as looking after the church's finances, she keeps our expectations in check when it comes to the Christmas wishes."

"I try, but it isn't easy. It breaks my heart when we have to say no." She leaned against the kitchen counter and frowned. "We've had to put a couple of requests aside. The most expensive wish was for a large mobility van. The community group who asked for it wanted to take injured military vets to the therapy pool in Polson. Their current van was donated, but it's constantly breaking down. We found a second-hand van for about twenty thousand dollars, but converting it to a mobility vehicle would have cost an additional twenty-five thousand. We can't afford that."

Peter knew what it was like for military personnel returning home with injuries. The never-ending financial, emotional, and physical obstacles they endured made their recovery difficult. If he could make one person's life easier, he'd do it.

"My company can't donate an entire mobility van, but I know some people who might be able to help." He smiled at Shelley's shocked expression. "If you could send me any information you have about the wish, I'd be grateful."

She took a business card out of her pocket and handed it to him. "If you email me your contact details, I'll make sure you have everything you need by tomorrow morning. If the people you know can't provide funding for the van, it's okay. Thank you for offering."

"I'll do my best to make it happen."

Shelley checked her watch. "If I don't take these apple pies into the dining room, everyone will have gone home before they see them." When Peter and Katie started to move, she held up her hand. "I'll do it. After your generous offer, I need to shake the adrenaline out of my body. John will be thrilled when I tell him you might be able to help."

"Umm, about that. If you could not mention my name, I'd appreciate it."

Shelley's eyes widened. "Oh. Is it because…" She glanced at Katie and cleared her throat. "Okay. I can do that."

Before Katie could ask what she meant, Shelley picked up two apple pies. "I'll be back soon."

After she left, Katie silently ate her dessert. When she looked at Peter, she had a frown on her face.

"You're awfully quiet."

"I'm thinking about what you offered to do. Most people wouldn't go out of their way to help people they don't know."

"I guess I'm not the same as most people."

Leaning forward, Katie scrutinized his face. "Why do you make prosthetic limbs?"

And just like that, she cut straight to the core of who he was. "We were already manufacturing high-tech mobility aids before we started the prosthetic side of our business. When I saw the archaic limbs most people are given after an amputation, I knew we could do better."

He lowered his spoon onto his plate. Katie deserved to know more than the generic answer he gave everyone. "I was in a relationship with a soldier whose right leg was badly damaged in a training accident. The doctors did everything they could to save it, but her lower leg had to be amputated. There was no funding for anything other than a metal pole with a shoe on the end."

When Katie didn't say anything, he sighed. "I sound bitter and twisted, and I don't mean to. I'm disappointed the health system can't fund better options for people who need help to live a good life."

"I don't blame you for being upset. Sometimes you need to have first-hand experience of how something *isn't* working before you can do anything about it. I never realized what it's like to be homeless, to crave a hot shower and a safe bed to sleep in until I started working with Pastor John. It made me realize how fortunate I am and how much I can do for other people. Is your friend okay now?"

He took a deep breath. This was the part he rarely discussed. The part that had left him heartbroken and full of guilt. "Sandy was devastated when she lost her leg. From the time she woke up in the hospital, she never came to terms with what had happened. Two years after the accident, she committed suicide."

"I'm sorry."

Peter pushed aside the cloud of grief that had snuck up on him. "She was a great person. I don't know whether one of our prosthetic legs would have changed what happened, but they're helping other people."

"Is the mobility van another way you can make a difference?"

"It's either that or penance. I used to beat myself up about not knowing how depressed Sandy had become. Before she died, my team was working on the conductive gel that makes the prosthetic limbs so effective. She was excited about what we were doing, but it wasn't enough to give her hope. If the van even makes a small difference in someone's life, I'll do everything I can to make it happen."

A lump formed in his throat when he saw the compassion and understanding in Katie's eyes. "Let's talk about something different. Have you tried formatting your manuscript?"

She smiled and nodded. "The software is amazing." With tears gleaming in her eyes, she brushed her lips against his. "Just like you."

Without knowing when or how it had happened, Peter felt himself falling into something special—and he never wanted it to end.

THE FOLLOWING EVENING, Katie rolled her eyes at Peter. "You can do better than that. Smile like you mean it." She held her cell phone higher, waiting for the moment he looked as though he was enjoying being dressed as one of Santa's Secret Helpers.

"It's all right for you," he moaned in a very non-festive way. "You like dressing up."

Dropping her hand, she sent him what she hoped was a

sweet smile. "It's Christmas. How do you think Santa feels? I'm sure he'd sooner be wearing jeans and a sweatshirt instead of the same suit he's worn for hundreds of years."

"He has an image to uphold." Peter straightened his red jacket and gave a resigned sigh. "I just hope the family we're visiting like our outfits."

"They will." Katie didn't have the courage to tell him Santa's other helpers only wore hats when they delivered the Christmas wishes. But, because it was her first year of helping, she wanted to do something special. Wearing the costume she'd worn at the Santa parade would make everyone happy. And when Ethan offered to lend Peter his elf costume, it seemed like their fate was sealed. Unfortunately, Peter had other ideas.

"Okay. I'm ready." With a smile that had probably won the hearts of many women, he waited for her to take their photo.

Not wanting to waste another moment, Katie lifted her camera and snapped not one, but at least six photos. She wouldn't get another chance to show everyone how cute he looked, so she wasn't missing this opportunity.

"Are you ready to deliver your first Christmas wish?" she asked him.

"I can't wait." This time, Peter's smile was genuine. "Do you know where we're going?"

Opening her truck door, she clambered inside. "The Skelseys live in the tiny home village. They're in house number eight. Benjamin asked for a computer so his dad could work from home."

"That sounds like a reasonable request. What does Benjamin's dad do?"

"He works at a call center in Polson. Over winter, the roads can close depending on how much snow we've had. When that happens, the company's happy for their staff to work from home. But the employees need to supply their own computer. Having one will mean Benjamin's dad can still work." She glanced at Peter, hoping he understood why this was so important.

"And a job means there'll be food on the table and the utilities will be paid?"

"Exactly." On the short drive from the church to the tiny home village, Peter asked questions about the village. She answered the ones she could and suggested he talk to Pastor John about the others. It wasn't until they arrived that she remembered to tell him about her books. "I spoke to my friend in Los Angeles. She'll upload my formatted manuscripts to all the e-book retailers."

"That will save you time. What about the covers?"

"I asked the children at The Welcome Center what they thought about my covers and they said they liked them. I also asked a friend who works at the local elementary school if she could show them to her students. Out of a range of books aimed at the same age group, they picked my covers as the ones they liked the best."

"That must have been a relief. Are you publishing any print versions?"

"A local printer already has the files. Because another person canceled their job, he can squeeze me in after Christmas."

"That's exciting."

She parked in front of the main entrance and sighed. "I wish it was. I'm scared no one will read my books."

Peter's eyebrows rose. "Are you kidding? Pastor John said the children at The Welcome Center love your stories. They said…" He stopped talking and looked guiltily through the windshield. "The snow has stopped falling. We should deliver Mr. Skelsey's computer before it starts again."

Katie studied the dull red blush creeping up Peter's neck. "What did the children say?"

"Nothing." He flicked off his seatbelt and leaped out of the truck. "I'll get the gift basket."

Shaking off her misgivings, Katie followed the long-legged elf with a red jacket and sparkly green shirt across the parking lot. For someone who hadn't known where they were going, he was figuring it out quickly.

CHAPTER 8

$\mathcal{K}$atie couldn't believe how quickly the last week had flown by. In between making sure the last of their pre-Christmas guests enjoyed their stay at the inn, she'd delivered more gift baskets and helped her family get ready for Diana and Ethan's wedding.

Whether it was wrapping the table favors, baking for the aunts, uncles, and cousins who would be staying with them, or making sure they had enough decorations for The Fairy Forest, it was a chaotic, frantic, and exciting time. At least with all the activity around her, she hadn't had a lot of time to worry about her books.

Today, everyone's focus was on getting the church ready for tomorrow's wedding ceremony. She stared at the balloon arch behind the area where Diana and Ethan would exchange their wedding vows. Instead of white or cream balloons, they'd chosen red and gold to match the Christmas theme.

Everything about the room was bright and colorful; from the flower arrangements their mom had made, to the small posies at the end of each row of chairs. If she was getting married, this was exactly the type of wedding she'd choose.

"I picked up the rose petals from the florist," Penny said. "Can you give me a hand to put them in the refrigerator?"

Taking one last look at the beautiful room, Katie turned to her sister. "Of course, I can. Where are they?"

"In the foyer. There are four boxes, but I'm hoping most of that is packaging and not the actual petals."

When she saw the boxes, Katie understood why Penny was so worried. The refrigerators in the kitchen were large, but she didn't know if the petals would fit. "Why did we order so many?"

"Mom was worried we didn't have enough, so she ordered extra."

That sounded like something their mom would do, especially when they'd only had a few weeks to organize the wedding. Carrying the four boxes between them, they walked into the kitchen. "I can't believe Diana's getting married tomorrow. It only seems like yesterday that Ethan proposed."

Penny smiled. "A four-week engagement wouldn't be most people's idea of planning ahead. So, when *you* meet the man of your dreams, set a wedding date that's at least a year in advance. I don't know if Mom will survive another whirlwind wedding."

"Especially straight after Diana's." As Katie squeezed a bag of petals onto a refrigerator shelf, Barbara raced into the kitchen.

"Have you seen Diana? She was supposed to be at Mom and Dad's place half an hour ago."

Katie frowned. "She isn't here. Maybe there was a holdup with the cake? Megan's been busy with all the Christmas things she's baking and may not have finished decorating it."

"I'll try Diana's cell phone again. Where else was she going?"

"To the dressmaker," Penny said. "But the appointment was two hours ago."

Katie looked at her sisters. "You don't think there was a problem with her gown, do you?"

"I have no idea." Barbara held her cell phone up to her ear. After a few seconds, she dropped it back into her pocket.

"No luck?" Katie asked.

"My calls keep going to voicemail. Why do we have so many petals?"

"Mom ordered extra." Popping the lid of the last box open, Penny sighed. "I don't think these will fit."

Katie pushed the bags that were already in the refrigerator across and squished in another couple of bags. "There's enough air in the bags to stop the petals from bruising." With a satisfying thud, she closed the door and turned to Barbara. "Why do you need to see Diana?"

"The candy canes she ordered have arrived, the lady who's doing our makeup wants to ask her a question, and Mom's in a tizzy. She thinks Diana's going to be a runaway bride."

After spending most of her life worrying about her daughters, their mom still couldn't relax when there was a big family occasion. "We've almost finished in the church," Katie said in the most positive way she could. "I'll call Megan to see if Diana's still at Sweet Treats. Where's Mom?"

"At her house. She's already baked two batches of chocolate chip brownies and four different flavors of cookies."

Their mom always baked when she was stressed. "At least she's not driving around Sapphire Bay looking for Diana."

"She made Dad do that." Barbara looked at her watch. "Daniella's expecting to see the entire bridal party in twenty-five minutes at The Fairy Forest."

Penny frowned. "Diana has a copy of the pre-wedding schedule. We should go to The Fairy Forest and wait for her there. If she doesn't turn up, then we panic."

Katie wrapped her arm around Barbara's shoulders. "Don't worry, Diana's never late for anything." At least, she hoped so.

PRINTING the final trial report should have given Peter a deep sense of satisfaction, but it didn't. The neural gel prosthetics had given each amputee significantly better physical, mental, and emotional outcomes than their previous prosthetics. But none of that would make a difference if he couldn't fund phase two of the project.

The expectations of the trial participants and the intense interest since the leaked information had hit mainstream media was overwhelming. A lot of people were depending on him, including the fifty-two people he employed.

A soft knock on his office door distracted him from the thoughts whirling inside his head.

Willow stood in the doorway, holding Tiffany. "I've just made a batch of muffins. Would you like one?"

"That sounds great. I'll come to the kitchen with you."

"Are you sure? If you're still working, I can bring one here."

Peter looked at his laptop and frowned. "It's finished."

"You aren't happy with the results?"

"I'm more than happy. It's all the work that comes next that's worrying me." Tiffany made a gurgling sound and he smiled. "It's probably less stressful than raising a child."

"A good friend told me to take one day at a time. Their advice worked better than cramming my head with the latest parenting advice."

He followed Willow down the stairs. The sound of Christmas carols grew louder as they approached the open-plan living area. This was the first year he'd been away from home for Christmas, and he wasn't looking forward to spending the time away from his parents.

Instead of focusing on what he was missing, he tried to stay positive.

"Are you enjoying being at home with Tiffany?"

"It's a big change. Half the time I have no idea what I'm doing and the other half I'm making educated guesses. From what I've worked out, as long as Tiffany has a clean bottom, a full tummy, and lots of sleep, we're okay." She kissed her daughter's forehead. "When she's a little older, I'll reopen my music studio. But, until then, I'm happy to spend my days here."

Peter stepped into the kitchen. The rich scent of chocolate muffins made him think of his mom. From the time they were babies, she'd stayed at home with him and his brother and sister. It wasn't until he was an adult that he realized how much she'd given up to look after them.

"You're a great mom, Willow."

"Thank you." Gently, she lay Tiffany in the crib Zac had made and tucked a blanket around her daughter. "Would you like hot chocolate, coffee, or sparkling water?"

"Hot chocolate would be great. I'll make it."

"In that case, I'll have a hot chocolate, too." She handed him two mugs from the cupboard and found a plate for the muffins. "You're really good with Tiffany. Do you want to have children?"

"I have to find a wife first. But, yes, I'd like to have a family." As he poured boiling water into their mugs, he tried to imagine having a baby. It was so far from the reality of his life, it wasn't easy. "You and Zac are the only people I know who have started a family. I'm amazed by what you do."

"Believe me, you'll learn fast. If you have any questions, you can always give us a call." Willow bit into her muffin and groaned. "These are delicious. I know you enjoy coming to Sapphire Bay. Have you thought about moving here?"

"It wouldn't be possible with the job I have."

"Why?"

An image of Katie filled his mind. Usually, he had a list of reasons why living somewhere else wouldn't work. This time, none of the issues seemed insurmountable, especially if it gave him more time with her.

He wouldn't have to stay here forever. Katie was moving back to Los Angeles in May and he could return to New York at the same time. But, with everything he needed to do, it was the absolute worst time to think about moving. "I need to be in New York to speak to the funders for the next phase of my project."

"You could fly back for a few days at a time. Besides, you've made a lot of friends here. You could stay with Zac and me. We have plenty of room."

"You wouldn't be looking for a free babysitter, would you?"

A mischievous grin lit Willow's face. "I hadn't thought of that."

"Well, just so you know, I'm happy to look after Tiffany— as long as you give me good instructions. But if I did move, I'd have to find somewhere else to live. You and Zac have been generous enough with your home."

"Don't worry about that. We enjoy having you stay." Willow looked thoughtful as she sipped her hot chocolate. "I could look for a rental for you. It's amazing what you can find when you already live here."

Peter's cell phone beeped and he read the text. "I have to make a call. I'll think about what you've said."

"Good. Tiffany will enjoy getting to know her Uncle Peter better."

He glanced inside the wooden crib and smiled at the sleeping baby. He'd enjoy getting to know her, too.

KATIE SLID her bridesmaid's dress over her head. In less than an hour, Diana would marry Ethan in The Connect Church.

From the moment her parents had arrived at the inn, it had been a whirlwind of activity. Between doing their hair and makeup, fixing dress and suit malfunctions, and fitting in something to eat, everyone was super excited about the wedding.

"Are you nearly ready?" Barbara yelled up the stairs.

"Coming!" Grabbing her shoes, Katie flew downstairs, hoping she hadn't missed Diana's grand entrance. Even after yesterday's rehearsal, her sister refused to tell anyone what her dress was like. Katie just hoped it was everything Diana had dreamed about.

Walking into the living room was like entering Santa's workshop. The enormous tree she'd bought from Ben was the only thing that wasn't moving. Her mom and dad were rushing around the room looking for someone's shoes. Barbara was putting the finishing touches on Penny's makeup, and Charlie, their beautiful Golden Labrador, was trying to eat the ribbons on his vest. If they weren't careful, he'd bump into the table holding all the Christmas gifts for their extended family and eat those.

"I'm here," she yelled to no one in particular.

"Have you seen Diana's shoes?" her mom asked. "She can't find them anywhere."

Katie looked around the room. "What do they look like?"

Her mom pulled out her cell phone and showed Katie a picture of white high-heels with pretty pink flowers on top. "She had them an hour ago, but she doesn't know where they've gone."

Katie looked down at Charlie. He didn't look particularly guilty, but that didn't mean he hadn't buried them in the garden.

"We've already checked his favorite holes," her dad said.

"And he doesn't have a drop of dirt anywhere on him," Barbara said as she applied another coat of lipstick to Penny's mouth.

Instead of looking around the living room, Katie walked into the kitchen. Although no one was in here, it was just as jam-packed as the living area. Except this time, it was full of holiday cookies and Christmas treats.

A heaviness settled in her chest as she looked at the gingerbread men they'd decorated. Last December, whenever she'd called her grandma, she was in the kitchen, preparing for Christmas. It didn't matter how many people were coming for a meal, there was always more than enough food for everyone.

Gingerbread men were her grandma's favorite Christmas treat. She'd spend hours decorating the spicy cookies with colorful frosting and sweet candy. Until Katie and her sisters graduated high school, each of the students in their classes received a crunchy gingerbread man before Christmas. It was a tradition Katie intended to keep when she had children.

"I wouldn't eat any of the cookies if I were you," Diana said from behind her. "Mom has a radar attached to her head and will know one's missing."

Katie turned around and stared at her sister. "Oh, my goodness. You look amazing." Diana's shy smile brought tears to her eyes. "Is that Mom's wedding dress?" The frilly, over-the-top gown she'd last seen before Barbara chose a wedding dress was gone. In its place was a gorgeous gown fit for any Christmas bride.

The puffy sleeves and fitting bodice were still there, but the pearl beads had been replaced with sparkly jewels. Instead of the heavy satin skirt, the bottom of the dress was almost entirely tulle. It was everything Diana had wanted.

Diana grinned. "I spoke to a friend of Mom's and she looked at the dress to see what I could do. I showed Mom the design and she was happy for me to go ahead with the changes."

"Has she seen the dress now that it's finished?"

"Not yet. I'm going to show everyone now."

"I found them!" Their mom rushed into the kitchen, holding Diana's shoes. "They were—" With a stunned expression, she stopped in the middle of the room. "You look so lovely."

Diana gave a relieved sigh. "I'm glad you like it. I was worried the changes would be too much."

Mabel hugged her daughter. "Don't be silly. The dress was gathering dust in a closet. I feel blessed that you wanted to wear it."

"Mom, do you want me to—" Penny rushed into the kitchen and almost ran into Diana. "Wow. Look at you."

"It's Mom's wedding dress."

Penny's eyes widened. "It's stunning. Wait here while I get Dad and Barbara."

Penny hurried into the living room. Within seconds, she was back with the rest of their family.

When their dad saw Diana, tears filled his eyes. "You look as pretty as your mom did on our wedding day."

Diana hugged him tight. "It must be the veil. It's the same one Mom wore."

"You look gorgeous," Barbara said. "I can't wait to see Ethan's face when you walk down the aisle."

Diana's eyes misted over. "I can't wait to see him, too. It feels like this is the beginning of the most exciting adventure of our lives."

Charlie flopped onto the floor beside Diana and everyone laughed.

"Well, maybe not the most exciting day for everyone," Penny added.

While Diana slipped on her shoes, Katie thought about the last eight months. Their grandma's death was the catalyst for the changes that had turned their lives upside down. At the time, she thought staying in Sapphire Bay was the worst thing she could do. But, looking back at everything that had happened, she was glad she was here.

Penny, Barbara, and Diana had fallen in love with men who adored them. They'd found a letter written by Abraham Lincoln in the drawer of an old dresser, and discovered more about their great-grandparents than they ever thought possible.

What was even more special to Katie was getting to know her sisters as adults. They hadn't lived together since they were in their late teens and, regardless of how much she hadn't wanted to stay, she was glad she had.

Her dad handed her a glass of orange juice. "You look as though you need this. Is everything okay?"

"I was thinking about this year and everything that's happened."

Her dad wrapped his arm around her waist. "I know you weren't happy about living here, but I'm glad you stayed."

"So am I. If it weren't for Grandma, we'd still be living in different cities and only seeing each other a few times a year."

"She had a way of drawing people together, even after she died."

Silently, Katie watched her sisters admire Diana's dress. The kitchen was filled with endless love, joy, and hope—all the things that were important to her grandma.

And maybe, if she focused on that, the next year would be better than the last.

CHAPTER 9

$\mathcal{P}$eter sat on an aisle seat and looked over the heads of the wedding guests at Diana and Ethan's wedding. When Katie told him her sister's wedding had a Christmas theme, he thought it was a nice way to include the festive spirit in their celebration.

What he hadn't expected was the way they'd woven the theme into the decorations inside the church. Garlands of pine, threaded with fairy lights, not only smelled sweet, but gave the church an instant Christmas makeover. Red and gold posies were tied to the last chair in each row, and vases full of flowers were dotted around the room. Even the Christmas carols playing softly in the background added something special to the day.

His gaze drifted across the room. Willow was standing on the far side of the church, taking photos of the guests before the bridal party arrived.

Tiffany made a gurgling noise and Peter looked into the stroller beside him. He sighed with relief when he saw she wasn't choking on anything. Zac and Willow would never forgive him if his first solo babysitting experience ended in disaster.

Tiffany's big blue eyes stared unblinkingly up at him. It must be his suit that confused her. For her entire life, she'd only seen him in jeans and T-shirts.

When he smiled, her face broke into a grin. Something inside of him melted when she recognized who he was. Instead of leaving her in the stroller, he leaned down and lifted her into his arms. If he was five months old, he'd want to see his daddy dressed in a suit with a sparkly red vest, too.

Pointing to the front of the room, he showed Tiffany her dad. Zac chose that moment to look at them. With a wave, he sent his daughter a tender smile.

Peter sighed. "Your daddy loves you, little one."

Tiffany gurgled and Peter reached for a muslin cloth, waiting for her lunch to explode over his jacket. When nothing happened, he relaxed against the back of his chair. Disaster number one had been averted.

The sound of trumpets heralded the beginning of the wedding march. As if sensing the guests' excitement, Tiffany's eyes grew even rounder than they usually were.

"It's okay," he whispered. "I'll hold you close so you can see Diana and her sisters. When you see Katie, give her an extra special wave. She's the petite red-head with curly hair." He turned toward the back of the church and stared at the woman who'd made him re-evaluate his life.

His heart pounded as her pale blue, sparkly gown drifted around her legs. As she moved gracefully down the aisle, she could have been walking on air. "There's Katie," he whispered. "Can you see how pretty she is?"

The lady sitting behind him smiled. There was something oddly familiar about her, but he couldn't work out what it was.

As Katie drew nearer, the sparkles on her dress turned to

snowflakes. He didn't know where she'd found her dress, but she was the most beautiful bridesmaid he'd ever seen.

Sending him a look that took his breath away, she continued down the aisle. Barbara and Penny followed, but he couldn't have told anyone what they were wearing. He had eyes only for Katie, and a heart that was just as captivated.

Twelve months ago, if anyone had told Katie she'd be dancing with the handsomest man in the room at Diana's second marriage, she would have told them they were crazy. But, here she was, floating around the dance floor at The Fairy Forest, feeling like the luckiest woman in the world.

Diana and Ethan's wedding ceremony was romantic, sweet, and filled with many thoughtful touches that would become wonderful memories. Even Charlie had woofed his approval as Pastor John had pronounced the happy couple husband and wife.

It wasn't until everyone arrived at The Fairy Forest that their family and friends really appreciated the theme of the wedding. When they saw the chocolate fountains, the candy cane chairs, and the canopy of twinkling fairy lights, they were speechless. Everything was bright, glittery, and magical —just like Diana wanted it to be.

Peter gripped her hand and they changed direction, avoiding a collision with her cousins. "Your mom's happy."

"She loves anything that brings our family together, especially when it means everyone's staying for Christmas."

"That sounds like my mom. Who's the lady on your right in the green dress with the purple shawl?"

Katie looked across the room and grinned. "That's my Aunt Beatrice. She lives in Florida with Uncle Oliver.

They're the most eccentric of mom's siblings. Did you notice the family resemblance?"

Peter tweaked a lock of her hair. "I wondered where your red hair came from."

"It's our Celtic ancestry. My great-grandparents immigrated to America from Ireland."

"They traveled a long way to get here."

"I'm not sure why they left, but it took more than two weeks for them to get here. It makes my move from Los Angeles seem like a stroll down the road." She looked thoughtfully at Peter. "When you come for Christmas lunch, I'll show you a copy of my great-grandmother's journals. She documented the entire voyage, along with her life after she settled in Montana."

His hold tightened around her waist. "Are you sure it's still okay for me to come to the inn? You have a house full of relatives."

"Are you kidding? I couldn't imagine the day without you. Zac, Willow, and Tiffany are coming. It'll be fun."

"In that case, I'd love to spend the day with you."

A bubble of anticipation made her grin. She'd always enjoyed Christmas, but this year would be special. "Have you spoken to your parents since they arrived in Montreal?"

"I talked to them this morning. Mom's enjoying spending time with her sister."

"That's good. Keeping in contact with your family is important. It wasn't until I came back to Sapphire Bay that I realized how many times I'd postponed coming here or put off calling my parents and sisters."

"Are you still moving back to Los Angeles?"

Katie nodded. Even though she was self-publishing her first six books, it didn't mean she wouldn't traditionally publish other books she wrote. "I think so. My agent's in California. I have a wonderful apartment and friends who do the craziest things." The song they were dancing to came to an end. Reluctantly, she stepped away from Peter. "I'll miss—"

Penny hurried up to them and grabbed Katie's hand. "Hi, Peter. I need my sister for a few minutes. Mom can't find the bouquet that Diana's supposed to throw."

Katie glanced at Peter and saw the disappointment in his eyes. "Can we talk later?"

"Sure. I'll be sitting with Willow and Zac."

With another tug pulling her away, she followed her sister across the room. Just thinking about the future made her stomach twist in knots. If she returned to Los Angeles, she would be following one dream and leaving another behind.

KATIE DIDN'T KNOW what it was about her sister's wedding but, by the end of the night, she'd felt overwhelmed with sadness. She should have been happy Diana had found an amazing husband. It was foolish to feel so down, but she already missed having her close.

At the moment, all her sisters were living in Sapphire Bay, working from the inn, and doing everything they could to fill the rooms with guests. But, once Katie returned to Los Angeles, the time they'd spent together would become a blurry memory.

"Is everything all right?" Peter sat beside her. His concerned frown brought fresh tears to her eyes.

"Ignore me. I've been like this after each of my sisters got married."

"It's not like you to be unhappy. Do you want to talk about it?"

She blew her nose. While everyone was enjoying the

reception, she'd found a sofa in an empty room where she could have a meltdown without anyone seeing her.

"This sounds selfish, but I'll miss Diana."

"It's not selfish. It's normal. My best friend got married last year. When I was standing at the altar with him, I kept thinking it was the worst day of my life."

"You did?"

"I wanted our lives to be the same as they were before he met Bianca. We used to hang out most weekends and eat too much junk food. If we felt like getting away from New York, we'd head to the nearest ski slope or find a great mountain bike trail. But, after he met Bianca, that changed and it's never been the same."

"Do you still spend time together?"

"We've been away for a couple of weekends and see each other at the gym. It isn't the same, but at least we spend some time together."

Katie dropped her head to her chest. "When I go back to Los Angeles, I won't see much of my family."

"I understand why you want to leave, but do you really need to live there?"

She looked into Peter's eyes and sighed. She could keep making feeble excuses, but they weren't the real reasons she had to return. "All my life, I've watched my sisters succeed in their careers. Penny's a hotshot property developer, Barbara's a social media consultant, and before Diana married her horrible first husband, she was training to be a teacher. Then I came along and decided I wanted to be a writer. And what's worse is that I can't even support myself from my writing. I'm twenty-eight years old and need to waitress to pay my rent and utilities."

"What's wrong with that?"

"Nothing—if you aren't from a family of overachievers. Even when I'm home, I'm the oddball. Penny's converting some cottages into small businesses, Barbara's still working with her clients from around America, and Diana's going back to college. They're doing all of that while juggling what needs to happen at the inn."

Katie took a deep breath. She was rambling, offloading all her frustrations on Peter but, now that she'd started, she couldn't stop. Throwing her arms in the air, she glared at him. "And what do I do? Bake. I bake cookies, pies, muffins, and cheesecakes. I make breakfasts and picnic lunches for our guests and dinner for my sisters. Anyone with half a brain could do that."

Peter's eyes crinkled at the corners. "I'm sure you have a whole brain, so you're already better off than most people."

"Are you laughing at me?"

"I'm trying not to."

Katie slumped against the wall. "If I'd published even one book with a publishing house, it would have made a difference. But, at the moment, I'm a wannabe author who has a career that's going nowhere. And do you know what the worst part is?"

"No, but I'm sure you'll tell me."

Katie shot him a suspicious stare. If there was even the remotest chance he was laughing at her she'd burst into tears. "The worst thing is that Charlie leaves the inn during the day, too. Ethan's taking him to the medical clinic for two hours each morning and afternoon. He said it helps his clients feel more at ease during their therapy sessions."

"Maybe you could look after him between times?"

She blew her nose and tried to pull herself together. "That's what Diana said. I'm sorry. You didn't leave the reception to listen to my problems."

"Do you feel better after talking to me?"

"I think so."

"Well, mission accomplished."

Katie took a deep breath. "You must be looking forward to going back to New York and seeing your friends."

Peter frowned. "I am, but I might not be home for long. I'm thinking of living in Sapphire Bay for at least six months."

Katie's mouth dropped open. "Why?"

"To find some balance," he said softly. "I've made good friends here. If I stay, I can catch flights home to see my family or for work."

"That will be a huge change."

"Not as much as what you and your sisters have done. If I don't like living here, I can easily go back to New York City."

Katie could only nod. It was bad enough thinking he was leaving in January, but saying goodbye would be even harder.

CHAPTER 10

*P*eter opened his truck door and took two boxes of gifts off the back seat. As he walked toward The Lakeside Inn, he admired its high-pitched gable roof, elegant columns, and festive decorations. It looked like the type of scene you'd find on a Christmas card. Even though he was missing his family, it was the perfect place to enjoy Christmas Day.

He wondered if Katie's family would be tired after the excitement of yesterday's wedding. Everyone had danced into the night, ate an endless supply of delicious food, and devoured mountains of creamy chocolate from the fountains.

If it hadn't been for Tiffany, he was sure he would have slept until mid-morning. But her plaintive cries at five o'clock had woken him out of a deep sleep and kept him awake.

"Peter's here," Mabel said excitedly as she opened the front door. "Goodness. What a lot of gifts."

"I brought extra in case I missed someone."

"That's very thoughtful. Did Willow and Zac follow you down the mountain?"

"They did. They're sorting out what needs to come into the house. After I've left the gifts inside, I'll go and help them."

Mabel patted her pocket before pulling out a cell phone. "We have plenty of family who can help. Barbara set up a family Facebook page. All I have to do is send a message to everyone and they'll come running."

Her prediction was scarily accurate. Within seconds, three teenage boys appeared at the top of the stairs.

"Come and give Zac and Willow a hand. They're unpacking their truck."

"They're parked behind Katie's blue truck," Peter added, in case they didn't know who they were looking for.

With a stampede of feet, the boys hurried outside.

"That will keep my sisters' grandsons busy for a few minutes." Mabel held out her hands. "Let me take a box off you. We'll leave the gifts under the Christmas tree."

When Peter saw the tree, he stopped and stared at the unexpected wonder. It was like a rainbow of light, glowing from the living room. Multi-colored baubles shone from beneath layers of red, pink, gold, and silver tinsel. He looked closer and saw strands of blue and orange hidden in the thick pine branches.

He remembered meeting Katie in the general store and seeing the basket of tinsel she'd bought. Looking around the room at each glittery surface, it was easy to see where it had gone.

"The room's beautiful, isn't it?" Mabel said. "Katie hung most of the decorations before the other girls gave her a hand."

"Your guests must love coming in here." The combination of fairy lights and decorations could have looked like a complete mess but, somehow, Katie had made it work. "I didn't realize Ben grew trees as tall as this one."

"He has some that are three times this size," Katie said from behind him. "Do you like it?"

"It's incredible." He smiled when he saw what she was wearing. A picture of Mickey Mouse dressed like Santa covered the front of her T-shirt. Beneath the image, the words, "T'is the season to sparkle," were surrounded by small, glittery beads.

Katie placed three gifts under the tree. "I found the T-shirt online."

"It's very Christmassy."

"That was the idea," she said with a smile.

Over the sound of Christmas carols, he heard the excited chatter of the boys returning from Zac and Willow's truck.

"Ho, ho, ho," Zac said happily from the entryway. He walked into the living room with a Santa hat on his head and his daughter in his arms.

One of the boys followed him with the stroller, which was laden with gifts. The other two were carrying containers of food and baby things.

"Put the presents under the tree and the food in the kitchen," Mabel said. "You might even find some cookies on the counter."

In double-quick time, the boys offloaded the presents and rushed into the kitchen. By the time Peter had placed his gifts under the tree, Mabel was holding Tiffany, and ten other people had joined them in the living room.

After Katie introduced everyone, she pulled him into the relative calm of the kitchen. The boys had disappeared somewhere, leaving the red-headed woman he'd seen at Ethan and Diana's wedding alone in the room.

Katie gave her a hug. "Aunt Beatrice, this is Peter Bennett, a friend of mine."

Beatrice wiped her fingers on a dish towel and shook his hand. "It's lovely to meet you, Peter. Merry Christmas."

"Merry Christmas to you, too. I liked the dress you wore at Diana and Ethan's wedding."

"Thank you. I made it a few days after we received the invitation. I love dressing up and a wedding's such a special time." A young girl squealed and Beatrice looked through the window. A group of children were building a snowman. "Help yourself to a cookie. I need to make sure everyone's behaving themselves."

Katie handed her aunt a jacket. "If you see any of my sisters, can you tell them to meet me in the kitchen?"

"I will but, if they don't show up, send a message on our Facebook group."

"I forgot about that."

"Your Mom hasn't," Beatrice whispered. "We might have to disable it after lunch."

Katie grinned at Peter. "I have the perfect person who can do that."

"Me?" He wasn't sure he wanted to upset Mabel.

"Apart from Barbara, you're the most techie person in the house. If anyone can crash a Facebook group, you can."

Beatrice opened the back door. "Or we could hide Mabel's phone. Being addicted to social media isn't good for anyone's health." And with those parting words, Beatrice left to check on the children.

Katie filled a tray with mugs. "I'm making hot chocolate. Would you like one?"

Peter sniffed the air. The sweet scent of melted chocolate filled his lungs and made him sigh. "That doesn't smell like the powdered variety."

"It isn't. This is the real deal." Katie lifted the lid on a saucepan and showed him the simmering liquid. "How does a drink made with melted chocolate, giant marshmallows, double-whipped cream, and a sprinkle of cinnamon sound?"

"Like heaven." His heart pounded when he saw her mischievous smile. "Apart from the hot chocolate, what's the best thing you like about Christmas?"

"Spending time with the people I love."

Peter brushed a lock of hair away from her face. "I feel the same way. Katie, I—"

"Oops. Sorry." Diana backed out of the kitchen. "Aunt Beatrice said you wanted to see me, but it looks as though you're busy."

A blush turned Katie's face as red as her hair. "Don't be silly. Peter and I were talking about hot chocolate."

Diana's eyebrows rose. "You were?"

"In a manner of speaking," Katie muttered. With a clatter, the lid of the saucepan landed on the counter. "Would you like some?"

"Is that why you wanted to see me?"

Katie frowned. "No. I wanted to tell everyone that Chloe called." She looked at Peter and her blush lost some of its super-red tone. "Chloe works at the Smithsonian Institute. Her team has been restoring the dresser where we found a letter written by Abraham Lincoln."

"And doing all kinds of things to the letter to make sure it doesn't deteriorate," Diana added. "Chloe's amazing. She's trying to find as much information as she can about our great-grandfather for an exhibition the Smithsonian's organizing."

Penny and Barbara walked into the kitchen.

"You want to see us?" Penny said.

"Chloe called Katie," Diana said to her sisters.

Barbara picked up a cookie and bit into it. "How is she?"

"She's good. Her family's having Christmas in Washington, D.C. this year, so it's making it a lot easier for her. But

99

that's not what I have to tell you. A member of her team thinks they're close to finding our great-grandfather's grave."

Barbara coughed. "How on earth would they discover that? We don't even know where he was living before he died."

Katie shrugged. "I have no idea, but the bereavement card we found helped. Chloe will email us everything they've found after they verify some of the information. She said it could take a few weeks."

Peter looked at each of Katie's sisters. Their expressions ranged from excited to totally confused.

Diana frowned. "I don't think we should tell Mom until we know for sure what they've found. It will only get her hopes up."

"That sounds like a good idea," Penny agreed. "Our great-grandfather was an interesting character. If he faked his death, his grave might not be real, either."

Katie handed Peter a cup of hot chocolate. "I'll tell you about our great-grandparents after lunch."

"Has Peter seen the replica dresser Ethan made?" Penny asked.

"Not yet." With a steadier hand than he could have managed, Katie poured the hot chocolate into the other mugs. "I'll show him the journals, too."

The door swung open and Mabel hurried into the kitchen. "Thank goodness you're all here. Is everyone ready for lunch?"

Penny wiped cookie crumbs off her shirt. "I'm more than ready. The smell of the food is making my tummy rumble."

"In that case, let's eat. Can someone tell Allan he needs to carve the turkey?"

"I'll do it," Peter offered.

Katie picked up the tray of drinks. "I'll go with Peter. I'll be back in a few minutes."

"Tell Beatrice to make sure everyone knows we're eating in ten minutes."

"I will." As soon as they were away from the kitchen, Katie smiled. "Everything will get a little crazy from this point forward."

"Because of the food?"

"No. Because we're all together."

Peter took the tray out of her hands and kissed her cheek. "There's nothing wrong with being a little crazy."

KATIE SAT beside Peter at the dining room table and opened her napkin. They'd had to bring extra tables and chairs inside to accommodate everyone but, listening to the noisy chatter going on around them, no one seemed to mind.

"Lunch looks amazing," Peter said. "Your family must have been up hours ago cooking all this food."

"We started at seven o'clock this morning. Between Wyatt and Penny's kitchen and ours, it's been like Grand Central Station."

"My parents usually take us to a restaurant for lunch. It's not as Christmassy as being here."

"Most years, we don't have an option about where we go for lunch. Everything in town is closed and we don't want to travel anywhere else. Tonight's dinner will be different. The church is hosting a big Christmas meal for anyone who wants to come. At four o'clock, we're loading the trucks with gifts and boxes of desserts and driving into town."

"Does that happen each year?" Peter asked.

"We've only been doing it since Pastor John arrived. The church's catering and hospitality class do all the baking for the main course and the rest of the community do the desserts and gifts. You should come. It's a great way to end the day."

"I'd like that."

If her smile was a little goofy, she didn't care. She enjoyed Peter's company and wanted to make each moment they were together count.

Her dad tapped his wineglass with a spoon. "Merry Christmas, everyone. On behalf of Mabel and I, I'd like to propose a toast." He cleared his throat and a hush fell across the tables. "This year has been one of the most extraordinary we've ever experienced. We've welcomed Wyatt, Ethan, and Theo into our family, felt the loss of Mabel and Beatrice's mom, and enjoyed the company of our daughters. The girls have transformed this beautiful home into an inn and created a thriving business. We've even had a mystery or two to solve when we found the dresser and discovered what was inside. Throughout everything, you have all been in our hearts and minds." He looked at Diana and Ethan and raised his glass. "To the newlyweds—thank you for delaying your honeymoon to spend time with us. It wouldn't be the same without you being here. And to everyone else—without your love and support, our lives wouldn't be as rich or rewarding. God bless and Merry Christmas."

Everyone raised their glasses and said, "Merry Christmas!"

Katie glanced at the photo of her grandma on the mantelpiece and her eyes filled with tears. Each Christmas after Granddad died, Grandma would wake at dawn and sit in her rocking chair, watching the sun rise over Flathead Lake. Katie would join her and they'd talk about Granddad and all the wonderful times they'd had with him.

Out of everyone in her family, it was her grandma who understood her the most. She was her soft place to fall and the one person who understood why she wanted so badly to publish her stories.

"Are you okay?"

She saw the concern in Peter's eyes and forced a smile. "I'll be all right. I was just thinking about my grandma. She would have loved being here."

"Maybe she is."

Peter's softly spoken words filled her heart with hope. As her family helped themselves to the delicious food, she lifted her eyes to the angel sitting on top of the Christmas tree.

Gathering all the love inside of her, she sent a silent prayer to the woman who'd loved her unconditionally, who'd always wanted the best for her, and never minded her late phone calls and excited chatter. But mostly, she thanked her for being her grandma.

CHAPTER 11

"Not charades!" Barbara groaned. "No one follows the rules and Dad always gives his team clues."

"You're supposed to have clues," Allan said stubbornly.

"But you aren't supposed to say them out loud. That's why it's called charades."

Katie laughed at the twinkle in her dad's eyes. He knew his flexible approach to the game annoyed Barbara, but that didn't stop him from wanting to play it.

"What if I promise to be less vocal?"

"It isn't possible," Barbara muttered.

Theo looked bemusedly from Barbara to her father. "I haven't played charades in years. It'll be fun."

"I can't believe you're agreeing with my dad."

Diana laughed. "There's a reason for that."

Barbara's eyebrows rose. "There is?"

"Bribery," Theo said without any sign of guilt. "Your dad promised to take me to his secret fishing spot once it gets warmer."

"Dad! That's not fair." Barbara's outrage only added to their dad's amusement.

Katie glanced at Peter. Before he agreed with Theo, she pulled him to his feet. "Count us out. I promised Peter I'd show him the dresser Ethan made."

"I'll come with you," Barbara said quickly. "At least that way I won't have to watch Dad bend the rules."

Theo held onto the back of her sweater. "You can't go anywhere. We need your general knowledge to beat your dad."

"You took a bribe from him."

"That doesn't mean I don't want to win. Between you, Aunt Beatrice, Penny, and your mom, no one else stands a chance of winning."

Mabel handed everyone in her team a notepad and pen. "Theo's right. We have the best team this family has ever seen."

That won Katie's mom a chorus of good-natured boos and laughter from the other family members vying for the title of Charade Kings.

Before anyone enticed Peter back into the game, Katie nudged him toward the guests' living room. "The dresser's this way."

Barbara gave a resigned sigh as they moved past her. "I can't believe you're abandoning me."

"It's for a good cause," Katie said with a grin. "Besides, Dad might have trouble beating Zac and Willow's team. They won the Christmas charades competition at the church."

A glimmer of hope appeared in her sister's eyes. "And they might stop Dad from giving everyone clues."

Katie didn't think anyone could do that, but she wouldn't spoil Barbara's newfound optimism. "Good luck. We won't be long." Holding Peter's hand, she led him into the adjacent living room. "When we remodeled our grandparents' home, we converted one of the living areas into a space our guests could enjoy and left the other one for us. So far, it's working well."

He looked around the heavily decorated room and grinned. "I can see why you needed all the tinsel. This room's even more colorful than the one we left."

A warmth spread through Katie as she absorbed Peter's smile. "I tried to make our living area as festive as possible. Even though we don't spend a lot of time in here, we wanted it to be special."

Peter stood in front of the replica dresser. "Is this what Ethan made?"

She didn't blame Peter for sounding so surprised. Very few people knew her brother-in-law was such a good furniture maker. "It's beautiful, isn't it? Usually, the dresser's in our guests' living room, but we moved it in here a couple of days ago." Katie opened the top drawer and handed Peter a folder. "We put some photos and information in this folder. A lot of people who stay here either read about the letter we found or saw one of the television stories about it."

Opening it to the first page, Peter studied the photo of the original dresser. "You wouldn't know this dresser isn't the original one."

Katie ran her hand over the gleaming mahogany case. "The real dresser has a few scratches and dents. Ethan didn't want to damage the wood on this one, so he polished it like a new piece of furniture. The brass handles are exact replicas of what's on our great-grandparents' dresser."

Peter turned to the next page and looked at the second photo.

"That's the drawer where we found the letter." Katie kneeled on the floor. "Ethan made a secret compartment, just like in the real dresser." Carefully, she opened the hidden drawer and handed Peter a sheet of paper. "This is a replica of a letter Abraham Lincoln sent to his son, Robert Todd

Lincoln. It contains the last draft anyone has found of the Gettysburg Address. The Smithsonian Institute has the original."

She enjoyed seeing the wonder on Peter's face. Her sisters had felt the same way when they'd realized what they were holding.

"How on earth did the letter end up in a dresser in your grandparents' home?"

"That's what we've been trying to figure out. Our great-grandmother's journals held some clues and Chloe at the Smithsonian has been amazing. Her team has spent weeks looking in places we don't have access to. From what we've discovered, it looks as though our great-grandfather, Patrick Kelly, faked his death to get away from his gambling debts. But that didn't stop him from visiting gambling houses throughout America. We think he met Abraham Lincoln's son in Chicago and won the letter during a game. A few months later, Patrick gave his wife the letter."

Peter inspected the hidden compartment. "She must have known how valuable it was."

"That's what we think, too. Before my great-grandmother died, she gave Grandma a key in a blue and gold snuffbox. She said as long as she kept it, she'd never need anything else. Grandma tried to find what the key opened, but it didn't fit anything in the house. After she died, we found the dresser in the old steamboat museum. She must have stored some of her furniture there when she was reorganizing her home."

"It was just as well you contacted the Smithsonian."

Katie thought about all the phone calls and meetings they'd had with Chloe and her team. "We wouldn't have learned about our great-grandfather's life without their help. On February 12 next year, the Smithsonian's opening an exhibition about the letter and our great-grandparents' lives."

"It sounds like something you won't want to miss."

"We're all excited. Chloe hasn't told us an awful lot about what her team's doing but, knowing her, it'll be fantastic."

Peter handed Katie the folder. "I can see why your guests want to stay here. Apart from sleeping in a beautiful house beside Flathead Lake, they get to experience some of the excitement of finding a forgotten letter."

"They appreciate us giving the original letter and dresser to the Smithsonian for safekeeping, too. We could have kept them or sold them to a collector, but it didn't seem right. Especially when our great-grandfather promised his wife he wouldn't gamble again."

"Did he ever return to Montana?"

Katie closed the drawer. "He came back to visit his wife and daughter, but we don't know how long he stayed. We found a bereavement card a friend of my great-grandmother's sent her. So, we know he died before she did but, until now, we didn't know where he was buried."

"Is that important?"

"I didn't think it would be until we found the bereavement card. We know a lot more about our great-grandfather's life than we did a few months ago, but there are still so many questions we can't answer. If someone in Chloe's team has found where he's buried, it would give everyone closure, especially Mom."

Peter wrapped his arms around her waist. "What if you never find where he's buried?"

"Mom will be a little disappointed, but we can't do anything about it. If we can't find his grave, we'll add something to my great-grandmother's headstone to commemorate his life."

"That's a good idea."

Katie leaned her head against Peter's chest. The sound of his heartbeat was strong and sure; it defined everything that had been missing in her life. "Do you have any deep, dark, mysteries in your family?"

"None that I'm aware of, but there are probably things someone doesn't want to share."

Leaning back, she smiled. "You could always create a little mystery of your own."

"The only unanswered question I have is why I didn't meet you sooner?"

"We haven't been in the same place at the same time, even in Sapphire Bay. After I arrived here, I spent most of my time remodeling the house and then cooking for our guests. When I wasn't doing that, I was writing."

"And I've mostly been at Zac's house and in the tiny home village, checking Richard's prosthetic leg." Peter kissed her forehead. "I'm glad I saw you in the general store."

"So am I." Katie snuggled closer. "Just imagine our lives if we hadn't met each other."

A roar of cheering erupted from the other living room.

"It definitely wouldn't be as exciting." Gently, Peter lifted her chin upward and kissed her so soundly that her knees almost buckled.

"My head's spinning," she whispered.

"I feel the same way. Do you think it means something?"

Pulling his head toward hers, Katie sighed. "It means we need to practice more."

And with a groan, Peter happily obliged.

THREE DAYS LATER, Peter looked at the sheet of paper in his hands, then at the cottage on Anchor Lane. The mailbox number, tilted so far sideways that it was a wonder it hadn't fallen off, told him he'd definitely stopped outside the right house, but he still hesitated.

After Christmas lunch, Katie had told him about the eight cottages Penny was remodeling. Four would become small businesses and the others would be transformed into family homes. From what he could see of the empty cottages, it wasn't a project for the fainthearted.

A window opened and a familiar face appeared. "Wyatt said you might be stopping by," Penny said as she jiggled the window wider. "I'll meet you at the front door."

He looked at the sagging porch, the blistered paint, and the rotten siding. He was surprised she'd been able to open the door, let alone use it to access the rest of the house.

"Welcome to our first commercial remodeling project in Sapphire Bay." Penny took off her yellow hardhat and grinned. "What do you think?"

"It's a beautiful building, but it'll take a lot of work to modernize it."

"We're keeping as much of the character as we can. Apart from a few new fixtures and fittings, replacing the porch, and removing a couple of walls, most of the work is cosmetic. Do you want to have a look inside?"

Peter nodded. He hadn't planned on going farther than the sidewalk, but he was intrigued by Penny and Katie's description of the cottages. Even though they were abandoned and falling apart, both sisters shared a vision of creating a row of successful small businesses and comfortable family homes.

As he stepped onto the porch, he watched where he placed his feet. "When did you start working on them?"

Penny handed him a hardhat from a box beside the front door. "I've had the keys since before Christmas, but I only started working on them yesterday. The construction team starts work on January 20. Watch out for the spiders and cockroaches."

Peter was surprised at how excited Penny was. "What is it about these houses that makes you want to remodel them?"

"They're part of the history of Sapphire Bay. Before it was a tourist town, these cottages were owned by the company that operated the steamboats out of Polson. They built them as vacation homes for their employees. Over the years, they've been used for lots of different things, but no one really knew what to do with them. When they were given to the county, they drew up plans to redevelop the properties, but that never happened." She stepped into the hallway and gazed up at the pressed tin ceiling. "With a lot of hard work, we can transform the cottages into homes and businesses that will change people's lives. I've worked on new multi-story residential developments and commercial buildings, but nothing's better than taking an old building and bringing it back to life."

Placing the hardhat on his head, Peter studied Penny's face. "I couldn't agree with you more. Did Wyatt tell you why I'm here?"

"You're planning a secret book launch for Katie. That's a really nice thing to do."

"I hope she likes it."

"After she gets over the shock, she'll love it. Katie was so disappointed when none of the publishing houses bought her books. Have you read any of her stories?"

"Not yet."

"When you do, you'll see why we're surprised no one wanted to publish them. She's such a good writer, but she can't see how wonderful her stories are." Penny stepped into another room. "This is the original front parlor. The fireplace is my favorite feature in this room."

The black fireplace, thick with cobwebs and dirt, was almost as impressive as the wide cracks in the wall above it.

"Are you sure it's safe to be in here? The chimney looks as though it's about to fall over."

"The construction crew will stabilize everything when they arrive. Out of the eight properties, only two have chimneys that don't need any work. But don't worry, it's perfectly safe."

Peter wasn't so sure. Taking a cautious step backward, he looked at the room's other features. If you ignored the peeling walls and a smell that was a cross between raw sewage and decay, it had potential. "Will this be one of the small businesses or a residential home?"

"This cottage and the next three will be businesses because they're the closest to Main Street. The other four will be rented as homes. Come and look at the rest of the cottage. It's bigger than it looks from the street."

By the time Peter viewed each room, he could see why Penny had worked hard to obtain approval for the redevelopment. With two large front rooms, a kitchen, a bathroom, and two more rooms that could become office and storage space, it would be perfect for a small business owner.

"Do the other buildings have identical layouts?"

"Right down to the same fireplaces and awful bathrooms. The last cottage is the only one that doesn't reek of sewerage." Penny smiled. "I noticed you're breathing through your mouth and not your nose. It's disgusting, isn't it?"

"A little." That was about the nicest thing he could say about the smell.

"Now I know why Katie likes you. You're diplomatic without being a pushover. Let's go outside while you tell me about the surprise book launch. If you need help with anything, let me know."

Peter was happy to step into the fresh air—even if it felt as though snow wasn't far away. With a relieved sigh, he left his hardhat in the basket and pulled out the spreadsheet he'd worked on last night.

As soon as she saw it, Penny sighed. "You're diplomatic and organized. Where did Katie find you?"

"In the general store by the display of tinsel." He laughed at the gleam in her eyes. "As strange as it sounds, I'm only organized because I have to be."

"Aren't we all? Even though Katie might look as though she lives her life spontaneously, she's as organized as the rest of us. She has to be to look after the guests at the inn, write books, and volunteer at the church. You'd be a perfect match."

A rush of heat hit his face. He'd thought the same thing a few times, but their future was so shaky that thinking beyond the next few months was hopeless. "You wouldn't be playing matchmaker by any chance, would you?"

"Who me?" she said in mock surprise. "I wouldn't dream of interfering in my sister's life."

That might be true, but he had a suspicion she wouldn't think twice about meddling in his.

PETER HAD NEVER GONE behind anyone's back before. Even though it was for a good reason, he felt slightly uneasy about not telling Katie what he was doing.

For the last few evenings, he'd worked alongside her, getting her website and retail accounts ready for her children's books.

When he wasn't working on his own projects, he'd checked with the local printer, coordinating everything that needed to happen to create print versions of her books. As far as Katie knew, there was a holdup with the printing and her paperbacks wouldn't be ready until the middle of January.

It was, of course, a litany of white lies and half-truths. Hopefully, she wouldn't be too upset when she saw how proud everyone was of her.

He looked around The Welcome Center and frowned. After he'd told Katie's family what he was doing, Mabel had coerced her family and friends into helping to decorate the meeting room for the book launch.

One group was hanging streamers from one side of the room to the other. Another group was in charge of the food and drink, and others had set up the tables and chairs.

Barbara and Penny were climbing two ladders, holding a banner between them.

"Lift your end higher, Barbara," Mabel said from the middle of the room. "That's it. Another inch should do it."

Megan, the part-owner of Sweet Treats, carefully walked into the room holding a large box. "Where would you like the cake?" she asked Peter.

He took her across to a table they'd decorated specifically for it. Once Megan slid the box into place and removed the cardboard, he looked closely at the design. It was much better than he'd imagined. "I can't believe you were able to replicate the cover of Katie's first book on the cake."

"I have a fancy machine that's like a color photocopier. It scans the image and prints it onto a special sheet of frosting. It was a little trickier creating the 3D effect, but it looks amazing."

Mabel stood beside the table and gasped. "Katie will be blown away by what you've done. Thank you so much, Megan."

"It was my pleasure, but Katie's graphic designer did all the hard work. All I had to do was make the cake look as good as her book. When will Katie be here?"

Peter glanced at his watch. "Her writing group will finish in about fifteen minutes. Are you staying for the book launch?"

"Unfortunately, I can't. I still have to finish a wedding cake. Give Katie a hug from me. It's amazing what she's achieved."

"I think so, too. Thanks for making the cake at such short notice."

"You're welcome."

After Megan left, Mabel hurried across the room to speak to Pastor John. While he had a few minutes on his own, Peter studied the rest of the food and drink.

With all the children from her writing group, their parents, and Katie's family and friends here to celebrate the book launch, it was a much bigger event than he'd thought it would be. But, as Mabel had reassured him, it wasn't every day an author publishes six children's books.

"Someone's been busy," Zac said.

He turned to his friend. "I'm glad you could make it. I think I've forgotten something, but I don't know what it is."

Zac looked around the room. "You have a table of Katie's paperbacks, lots of food and drink, a cake, banners, and balloons. I don't think there's anything else you could add except the author."

"She'll be here soon."

Diana walked into the room with Charlie. Even from where Peter stood, he could see the Golden Lab's twitching nose. It was just as well he was on his leash. Otherwise, the food table would have been ambushed.

Zac patted his shoulder. "I feel like I'm your best man, waiting for your bride to walk down the aisle."

"I'm nervous," Peter admitted quietly. "What if this isn't what Katie wants?"

"Who wouldn't want to celebrate their books being published?"

"You're probably right." He wanted Katie to see just how proud her mom and dad were of her. They didn't see her writing career as a failure or a complete waste of time. Whenever he saw Mabel, she was telling someone about Katie's stories. She was her biggest advocate and a proud mom.

Allan joined them. "My baby girl will be stunned when she sees what you've done, Peter. It was a great idea."

"As long as she likes it, I'll be happy."

Allan sighed. "Katie didn't want us to make a fuss when her books were published. It's been so long since she finished the first story that I think the thrill has worn off. But, knowing my daughter, she'll be excited when she sees what you've done."

Taking a deep breath, Peter tired to calm his nerves. In fifteen minutes, everyone would know how Katie felt about the book launch.

CHAPTER 12

*K*atie opened the box she'd brought to the children's writing group. Although it wasn't an official meeting, everyone was here, talking about what they'd done on Christmas Day and their favorite gifts from Santa.

Katie smiled as Adele showed Nora her new doll's curly blond hair and big blue eyes.

"She looks like you," Nora said with a grin. "What's her name?"

"Dolly. Mom said I could take her to school."

"You should make sure your teacher looks after her when you're not there. Otherwise, she might get lost."

Adele frowned and hugged Dolly close to her chest.

After those words of warning, Katie thought she'd better change the subject. She cleared her throat to get everyone's attention. "Before you go home, I have something special for everyone."

Each child's eyes focused on the plate of cookies sitting in the middle of the table.

"No. It isn't the cookies. I have something special in this box."

"Is it a kitten or a puppy?" Charlie asked.

Katie shook her head and Charlie sighed. He'd wanted a pet for as long as he'd been coming to the writing group. When he found out Diana's dog shared his name, he was even more determined to talk his mom into adopting a shelter animal.

"Do you remember when we talked about your books and how we could share them with everyone?"

Andy looked at the box. "Did you photocopy our stories?"

"This is better than a photocopy." Katie took one of Andy's books out of the box. The glossy paperback cover was exactly as he had drawn it. "This is your book." As soon as the children saw the paperback, they crowded around the table.

As he turned the pages, Andy's eyes widened. "It even has the drawings I made. They look great."

She was glad he liked it. "Have a look in the back of the book."

He flicked to the last page. A few weeks ago, Katie took photos of each child to add to their author biography in the back of their handmade books. What they didn't know was that the same photos would be part of the paperback versions of their stories.

"It's like a real book."

Katie smiled. "It is real." Reaching into the box, she pulled out a copy of each child's book and handed it to them.

When Nora saw the picture she'd drawn of Marley, the dog who could jump as high as a horse, she ran across to Charlie and showed him the cover. "Look, Charlie. It's my book."

With a grin, he showed her his book.

There was so much excited chatter that Katie knew she'd done something none of the children would forget.

"Can we take them home?" Nora asked.

"Of course, you can. I asked the printer to make five copies of each book so you have copies you can give to your family and friends."

Andy looked in the box. "Where are your books?"

"They'll be printed in a few days. As soon as I have them, I'll bring them to one of our meetings."

Adele wrapped her arms around Katie's legs. "Thank you. Mom and Dad will love my book."

"I know they will. Mindy Mouse is the cutest, most amazing mouse I've ever met."

"And she likes chocolate," Adele whispered.

After more hugs and lots of smiles, the children ate their cookies and admired each other's books.

As she looked around the room, a knot of sadness settled in Katie's chest. She'd miss each of the children when she returned to Los Angeles. Even though they hadn't known each other for long, they were an important part of her life. They inspired her to write, to create something they'd enjoy reading. But, most of all, she loved seeing the way they supported each other, no matter what they were doing.

Today was one of the best afternoons they'd had together, but it was time to leave. She'd promised Pastor John she'd meet him in his office at five o'clock and it was almost that now.

Unlike her, the children were super-excited and full of confidence when their parents and caregivers arrived to pick them up.

After everyone had gone, she gazed at the empty room. Eight months ago, she was determined not to live in her grandparents' home for a year. Now she was wondering how she could ever leave.

❄

PETER CHECKED HIS WATCH, then looked around the room. All of Katie's family and friends were here. Even the children from her writing group were waiting quietly beside their parents. It wasn't until they'd arrived in the room that they were told why they were here. And, from the expressions on their faces, they were just as excited as everyone else.

"Have they left John's office?" Barbara asked.

Peter glanced at his cell phone. Pastor John was going to text him when they were on their way. "Not yet. All of Katie's writing group are here, so they must be arriving soon."

"I can't wait to see her face when walks into the room. Katie won't know where to look first."

He hoped she didn't think they'd gone overboard with the decorations. Between the balloons, banners, and a mountain of food, no one could imagine anything other than a party was happening here tonight.

When his cell phone buzzed, his heart pounded. In a voice that was as loud as he dared, he said to everyone, "They're on their way."

An expectant hush fell across the room and everyone turned toward the doors. It seemed to take forever but, eventually, John opened the door.

"I think this might be too big for what you..." Katie stepped into the room and her voice dropped to a whisper. When she saw everyone smiling at her, her eyes widened.

"Surprise!" Mabel shouted from the far side of the room.

Katie's family and friends erupted in applause and congratulations filled the air. It wasn't until Diana hugged Katie and whispered something in her ear that she finally looked a little less shell-shocked.

When her eyes connected with Peter's, he walked up to her. "We wanted to celebrate the publication of your books. Congratulations."

Katie looked over her shoulder, then pulled him close.

"My books won't be ready until the end of next week," she whispered in a panicked voice. "Even my e-books aren't loaded onto the retail sites yet. What will I tell everyone when they want to see my books?"

"You'll tell them to follow me."

Her panic turned to confusion, especially when she saw thirty-four sets of eyes staring at her. "What do you mean?"

Peter held her hand and walked to the other side of the room.

As soon as Katie saw her books, her mouth dropped open. Slowly, she picked up one of the books and opened it to the front page. "It's perfect." Lifting tear-filled eyes toward him, she said, "How did you do this? There was a problem with the printer and—"

"There was nothing wrong. I wanted to surprise you with your very first book launch. Since your aunts and uncles are still here after Diana's wedding, it seemed like the perfect time to celebrate what you've achieved."

Hugging the book close, she looked around the room. "Thank you all for coming. This is a big surprise. I never imagined..." Taking a deep breath, she started again. "I never imagined having a book launch, but I'm really glad you're able to see my books." She bit her bottom lip and silently pleaded with Peter to say something.

"We're happy to see them, too. Before we look at them and enjoy the delicious food, your mom wants to say something."

Mabel hurried across the room and hugged Katie tight.

When he heard the softly spoken words of encouragement she whispered in her daughter's ear, he knew this was the right thing to have done.

Stepping away from Katie, Mabel wiped her eyes and pulled a piece of paper out of her pocket. "I've been waiting for this moment since you were eight years old and told me you wanted to write a book."

The sound of good-natured chuckles filled the room.

With a wobbly smile, Mabel continued. "Your dad and I always knew you were special. Even when you were a little girl, you had the most inquisitive nature of any of your sisters. You asked so many questions and spent hours daydreaming about the answers. You've worked so hard for this. Through high school and college, waitressing and cleaning jobs, you've kept writing, kept pushing for your books to be published. And now they are, we couldn't be prouder. Instead of letting someone else do the process for you, you've found your own way of achieving your goals and that takes more courage and commitment than anyone can imagine. So, on behalf of everyone who's here, I want to say congratulations. And just so you know, we're looking forward to book seven, so don't take too long to finish it."

Lots of smiles and hand-clapping followed Mabel's speech.

"Don't forget the cake," Penny said from behind her mom.

"I knew there was something else we had to do," Mabel murmured. Turning Katie around, she showed her the cake Megan had made.

It didn't take long to see the delight on Katie's face. "It's amazing, but it's too lovely to cut."

Allan stood beside his daughter and handed her a knife. "Don't worry. I've taken lots of photos. All I need is one of you cutting the cake for the community Facebook page." He smiled at the embarrassed look in her eyes. "Your mom insisted."

With a soft sigh, Katie held the knife against the cake and smiled at her dad. After another round of applause, everyone moved toward her, wanting to hug her and offer their own congratulations.

Peter moved to the side of the room. Despite Katie's surprise, she seemed much happier now that everyone was talking and enjoying each other's company.

He watched the children from Katie's writing group crowd around the table, looking at her books with their parents. He smiled when a little girl left the table to wiggle through the adult legs to give Katie a hug.

"That's Adele. She lives at The Welcome Center with her mom."

Peter turned to Pastor John and took the piece of cake he handed to him. "Thanks."

"I didn't want you to miss out. Adele talks non-stop about what they do in the writing group. Even though she's only six, she loves being around Katie and the other children."

Peter was surprised she was able to be part of the group. "Does she write her own stories?"

"She tells her mom her stories and she writes them for her. After they've done that, Adele draws all the pictures and places them in the text. Have you seen the books Katie printed for her group?"

"She said she was doing something special for the children, but I didn't know what it was."

"That sounds like Katie. She does a lot of things no one knows about." John pointed to an older boy clutching a book. "That's Andy. You might have met his mom, Andrea. She works at The Welcome Center. Anyway, Andy entered a writing competition and won. Without Katie's encouragement, I don't think he would have entered anything. If you get a moment, take a look at his book. Katie showed it to me a few days ago and it's incredible."

Peter finished the piece of cake John had given him. "They'll miss Katie when she goes back to Los Angeles."

"They won't be the only ones."

Shelley, John's wife, joined them. "What a wonderful way

to celebrate Katie's books. She's glowing from all the compliments and, to make it even better, we've sold most of the books we brought to the launch."

Peter studied the happy faces around him and felt a weight lift off his shoulders. Katie was enjoying herself and her family and friends were showing her how proud they were of what she'd accomplished. If that didn't give her confidence a boost and make her feel as valued as her sisters, he didn't know what would.

AN HOUR LATER, Katie picked up what was left of the cake and carried it into the kitchen. Tonight had been both wonderful and terrifying. With so many people looking at her books, she was sure someone would say they didn't like them. But the only complaint was that none of the copies were signed. After twenty minutes of adding her signature to the front pages, she'd finally finished the last book.

Peter looked up from the dishwasher. "How's your hand?"

She flexed her fingers and winced. "Cramping. I'm not used to being famous."

He grinned and took the knife off the cake board. "You'd better get used to it. Before you know it, David Walliams will be inviting you on his podcast to talk about children's literature."

"I didn't know he had one."

"Research," he whispered as he leaned toward her. "It opens the door to opportunities you never thought were possible."

"Is that what you tell your staff before they start a new project?"

"Sometimes. Tell me, what does a world-famous children's author do in a small Montana town on a Friday night?"

Katie grinned. "She helps load dirty dishes into the dishwasher, then cleans up the tables from The Welcome Center's community dinner."

He looked around the bustling kitchen. "A lot of people are helping. We could disappear without a trace and no one would notice."

"Or we could give everyone a hand for half an hour, then leave." Carefully, Katie slid the cake onto the counter, then pulled a cart of dirty dishes over to Peter.

While they were celebrating her book launch, the dining room was full of people enjoying a free hot meal.

The volunteers who provided the dinners worked incredibly hard to give everyone a healthy and tasty meal. They didn't need the dishes from the book launch adding to their busy evening.

Peter picked up two more plates and slid them into the dishwasher. "You're too good for my humble soul."

"There's nothing humble about you, Peter Bennett. You'd ruffle many young women's feathers if you put your mind to it." Opening the door of another dishwasher, she pulled out the tray for the cups and glasses.

"The only feathers I'm interested in ruffling are yours. When we've finished here, do you want to grab something for dinner? We could go back to Zac's house and eat it there or have something in town."

She looked through the kitchen window and scowled. With icy roads and snowdrifts galore, it wasn't the best time to go anywhere at night. "How about we have dinner at the inn? I cooked a yummy beef casserole with herb dumplings, mashed potatoes, and green beans for dinner. Even after my family has eaten, there should be lots of leftovers."

"That sounds better than a cheeseburger and fries."

Katie nudged him with her hip. "I hope so. Thank you for what you did tonight. I wasn't going to do a book launch."

"That's what worried me. When your parents said you didn't want to make a fuss, I thought this might be too much."

"It was perfect." She wrapped her arms around Peter and gently kissed him. "I'll remember tonight forever."

His eyes crinkled at the corners as he smiled. "I hope there are many more memorable moments in our lives."

With a sinking feeling, Katie hugged him close. In a few months, they'd be living on opposite sides of the country. It didn't matter what they said or did. There would never be enough time to create memories that would last a lifetime with this wonderful man.

CHAPTER 13

*P*enny tapped her pen against the side of her coffee mug. "I know it's New Year's Day and you have things you want to do, but can everyone stop talking and concentrate on our meeting?"

Barbara grinned from the other side of the table. "While we were at Mom and Dad's apartment last night, a little birdy told me you and Wyatt are ready to start a family."

Katie stared at Penny. It didn't surprise her that she wanted to have a baby, but she'd only been married for a couple of months. "Are you sure?"

Penny rolled her eyes. "I wouldn't have married Wyatt if I wasn't. Apart from anything else, I'm nearly thirty-five years old. If we don't start trying soon, it might be too late."

"Mom didn't have me until she was almost thirty-six," Katie reminded her. "And I turned out okay."

"You're the baby of the family. Mom and Dad already had us before you were born." Penny sighed. "This isn't supposed to sound mean, but I don't have to tell everyone what's happening in my life."

"Yes, you do," Katie said. "We're sisters."

"Who won't have a business if we keep talking about babies." With a lethal stare, Penny handed Barbara, Diana, and Katie a copy of their planning schedule. "From this Thursday, excluding when we go to Washington, D.C., we have a full house of guests through to the beginning of September. That leaves us with a big question mark over who will organize our guests' breakfasts after Katie flies to Los Angeles."

"We could ask Kathleen from Sweet Treats," Diana suggested. "She only works in the afternoons. She might be happy to provide breakfast for our guests each morning."

"You'll need someone to make picnic lunches and the occasional dinner, too," Katie reminded Penny. "I have a folder of recipes that are quick and easy to make. I could leave that for whoever helps."

Charlie, their Golden Lab, sat beside Diana. Her hand automatically lowered to scratch behind his floppy ears. "Do you really need to leave? I was hoping that once you'd published your books, you might want to stay."

"What about Peter?" Barbara asked. "Zac said he's staying in Sapphire Bay for at least another six months."

Katie crossed her arms in front of her chest. "Peter's staying here, but I promised my boss I'd return in May."

"But you've already published your books and it's so much cheaper living here."

Everything Barbara said made perfect sense, but there was still a part of Katie that wanted to sell books through a traditional publishing house. She knew she could do it. It was just a matter of having the right manuscript for them to look at.

Diana touched her shoulder. "Why do you still want to go to Los Angeles?"

Katie looked at each of her sisters, worried they'd think

she was foolish. "When I moved to California, I told everyone I would get a publishing contract."

"And you think because that hasn't happened, you've somehow let everyone down?"

"No. Not being offered a publishing contract makes me feel like a failure," she admitted as tears clouded her eyes.

"You're not a failure," Diana said firmly. "You don't have any control over whether someone likes your books or not. It's their loss if they can't see how good your stories are."

Katie dropped her hands to her lap. "I know that and I'm incredibly grateful for everyone's help. I'm blown away by the number of sales I've made, but that doesn't change how I feel. My first six books weren't the ones that were going to secure a contract, but the next one might."

Penny frowned. "And if it doesn't?"

Katie didn't want to think about what would happen if moving back to Los Angeles was a waste of time. Especially if it meant saying goodbye to Peter.

Diana picked up her copy of the spreadsheet. "Katie needs to decide what she's doing, so let's give her the time and space to do that. In the meantime, we need to work on plan B. Finding a potential replacement for her in the kitchen is important. If we don't have any firm contenders, we'll have to advertise."

"And the sooner we do that, the better. But just for the record, we'll miss you, Katie. If there's any chance you'd consider staying, do it. If not for us, for Charlie."

Charlie's ears twitched when he heard his name.

"He's waiting for the W word." Diana smiled when her canine buddy looked imploringly up at her. "We'll go for a walk later. And if we're really lucky, Katie will come with us."

With a heartfelt sigh, Charlie lowered his head to his paws.

Katie wished her needs were as simple as Charlie's. He

loved running in the forest and jumping in the lake. If she could find the same contentment, her life would be so much easier.

Penny tapped her pen against the table. "The next issue we have to discuss is Valentine's Day. Theo wants to organize a competition through the radio station, with the first prize being a four-day stay at the inn. What does everyone think?"

"It's a great idea," Barbara said. "Tell us more."

As Penny summarized what Theo's listeners would need to do to enter the competition, Katie thought about returning to Los Angeles. If moving here was a big deal, leaving would be harder. She really needed to talk to Peter and find out how serious he was about staying. And then she needed to call her agent. If there was no hope she'd ever receive a contract, then her decision would be easier than she thought.

THREE DAYS LATER, Peter read the list of names Pastor John had given him. Each of the teenagers was short-listed for the college scholarships BioTech was sponsoring. "I think I met Nate and Marcus at the Christmas Tree Farm."

"That wouldn't surprise me. They're there most days after school and on the weekends. Nate's mom had an accident a while ago and he was working three part-time jobs to pay their bills. Ben saw a lot of potential in him. He gave him more hours so he didn't have to split his time between the different jobs."

"What's Marcus' background?"

"He moved here from Polson when he was younger. A few interactions with the police didn't give him the best start, but he worked with a counselor and completed our youth employment program. Since then, he's gone from strength to strength."

Peter looked at John. "Do they want to go to college?"

"They've already applied for scholarships, but they missed out."

He read each of the profiles, seeing the similarities between these teenagers and his own life before he went to college. "You've mentioned that Nate makes hand-carved toys for The Christmas Shop?"

"That's on top of helping on the farm and serving in the shop."

"Is that why he wants to study sculpture and extended media?"

"It is. He's a clever kid. Marcus, on the other hand, is interested in cyber security. One of the police officers he met took him under his wing. I'm not sure whether the idea of getting into computer security came from that relationship or from his interest in programming but, either way, he'll never be out of work. The other three teenagers have come from a variety of backgrounds and have different goals. One day, they'll make a difference in the world. All they need is the opportunity to shine, and a college degree would help make that happen."

"They sound like ideal candidates." Peter handed the folder back to John. "Has Shelley spoken to my staff?"

"She has. Everything's organized. Montana State University is happy to fit in with BioTech's requirements and the needs of the students. It was generous of you to include a travel allowance for each scholarship."

"Bozeman isn't too far away, but it can feel like you're in a different country if you can't get home."

"What about you?"

"Me?"

John smiled. "I heard you're staying in Sapphire Bay for six months. That's a significant change."

"It is for me. I've lived in New York for most of my life." Peter wondered if there was any news that didn't make its way around town. "How did you know I was staying?"

"Zac said something to Diana, she told Mabel, and now everyone in Sapphire Bay is looking forward to meeting you. Have you found somewhere to live?"

"Not yet. Katie said she'd help me look this weekend."

"Well, if you get stuck, you can always stay with Shelley and me. We have plenty of spare bedrooms."

"Thanks for the offer, but I should be okay. I'm heading back to New York to sort out some issues, so there's no hurry."

"It might be more difficult than you think to find accommodation. There aren't many rental properties around the lake, and buying a house can be almost as difficult. Penny might have some ideas."

"Katie said the same thing. Zac knows a realtor who might be able to help, too."

"It sounds as though you've covered all your bases. Before you go, I've got something else to show you." Reaching across his desk, he handed Peter a folder. "It's a list of the programs the church will be providing because of your generous donation. Shelley's documenting the objective of each program and how we'll measure their success. I'll send everything through to your office when it's finished."

Peter looked at the list. "I've heard a lot of good things about the programs the church runs, but I didn't realize how many there are."

"We focus on programs that enhance the educational, social, and emotional wellbeing of the community. For us, each activity is as important as the others. It doesn't matter whether it's the drop-in support group for veterans or the hospitality and catering class; each program gets what it needs to be effective."

From what he'd seen, it had done more than that. Even Katie's writing group did so much more than teach children how to write. She'd created a safe and nurturing environment for their growing minds to flourish. And if anyone thought that was easy, they hadn't worked with children.

They both turned when someone tapped on Pastor John's office door.

"Great, you're still here." Andrea handed Peter a slip of paper. "Katie asked me to give you this."

"She was here?"

"About five minutes ago. She had to leave, but she said to text her if you want to see this house this afternoon. It's available as a rental and won't last long."

He read the address and frowned. He had no idea where 15 Cherry Blossom Lane was but, if it was in town, he'd take almost anything. "Thanks, Andrea."

"Good luck." She smiled at Peter and John, then left the office.

"That was good timing."

Peter slid the piece of paper into his pocket. "I'll remember what you said about not having a lot of choice when I view the property."

"Keep an open mind. It's amazing what a coat of paint and new curtains can do for a house."

Peter laughed. "You sound like Katie. She's always adding new cushions or moving furniture around at the inn."

"It must have something to do with her creative mind."

"Or that she likes change." He only hoped she didn't want to change where she was living. Los Angeles might have bright lights and literary agents, but so did New York City. If Katie wanted to pursue a traditional publishing contract, she'd be better joining him in Manhattan.

But he'd already mentioned that to her and her answer was as determined as ever. She had her heart set on returning to California, and nothing he said would change her mind.

KATIE COULD HARDLY CONTAIN her excitement. Cherry Blossom Lane was such a pretty street that people came here just to enjoy the trees and the wonderful old houses. When she'd heard the owners of her favorite home wanted someone to rent it, she'd immediately thought of Peter.

As soon as she saw him, she leaped out of her truck and threw her arms around his neck, giving him a hug. "I'm glad you could make it."

"I was in town, so it was good timing." He kissed her before looking over her shoulder. "Is this the house that's perfect for me?"

Katie nodded. "It is. I know we weren't going to look at anything until the weekend, but a friend of a friend wants to rent their house while they're living in Switzerland. I haven't been inside, but I've walked past it lots of times. Isn't it amazing?"

Peter's gaze swept across the two-story house's wooden siding, the bright red front door, and the wide porch with gingerbread trim. "It's an impressive home."

"Shona, my friend, said it has four bedrooms, three bathrooms, and a double garage. You could use one bedroom as an office and still have two spare rooms for your family when they visit. The owners are leaving their furniture, so you wouldn't have to buy anything."

"It sounds great. Do we need to wait for a realtor?"

Katie shook her head. "The owners, Mr. and Mrs. Princeton, left the front door open. They've gone into town to buy some groceries while we look around."

"They're very trusting."

"I've met them a few times in the general store. As long as I text them before we leave, everything will be okay. If you want to rent it, they'll meet us here and discuss the paperwork."

Peter opened the wrought-iron gate. "In that case, I'll follow you."

Katie had to stop herself from running ahead. Apart from slipping on the icy path, she didn't want her enthusiasm to influence his decision. "The garden will take a little maintenance but, if you're only here for six months, it won't be too bad."

"When do the owners leave?"

"In two weeks." She stepped onto the porch and had to stop herself from sighing. She could imagine Peter waking up early and sitting on the swing, enjoying an early morning cup of coffee before the rest of the world stepped out of bed.

Peter sent her an amused glance. "I have a feeling your imagination's working overtime. I'm only renting the house, not buying it."

"I know, but I love everything about this street. When I was growing up, I used to daydream about what it would be like to live here. Mom and Dad's house seemed so boring compared to these ones." Taking a deep breath, she opened the door and stepped inside. Clamping her lips together, she tried not to show Peter what she thought of the high ceilings, the wide hallway with its sparkly chandelier and paneled walls, and the ornate mirror reflecting the sunlight streaming in from a bedroom.

"It's nice and big."

"It's glorious," she murmured. "The moldings and cornices

must have been part of the house when it was originally built." Everywhere she looked, Katie found something to enjoy. She didn't know whether remodeling her grandmother's house gave her a better appreciation of this house, or if it was simply stunning but, either way, she was in awe of the lovely old building.

Peter walked into one of the front bedrooms. On the far side of the room, a set of doors led into a large master bathroom and a walk-in closet. "The owners have done an amazing job of remodeling the house. They've modernized it without losing any of its character."

"Does that mean you'll rent it?"

He tapped the end of her nose. "It means I'm impressed. Let's look at the kitchen."

Following the hallway to the back of the house, they found the kitchen on the right-hand side of an open-plan family and dining area.

Peter stood in front of a set of French doors. "It looks as though this area was added on a few years ago. It looks good."

Katie ran her hand along the stainless-steel counter. If she owned the house, she'd replace the counters with granite or quartz, paint the brown cabinets white, and add bright yellow pendant lights over the island. But she wasn't buying it and, even if she was, she didn't have enough money to do any remodeling.

Peter looked inside the pantry. "There's plenty of storage and the appliances are fairly new. I like it."

"Enough to live here?"

Peter smiled. "Enough to live here."

Her heart leaped in her chest. "I'll text Mr. and Mrs. Princeton. They'll be happy it'll be looked after by someone who's reliable. Do you want to know how much it costs?"

"It doesn't matter."

Katie's eyebrows rose. "It could be more than you want to pay. I'd hate you to get your hopes up and then have to—"

"It's all right. I'm paid more than enough to rent the house."

"Oh." Before she wondered how much money Peter earned, she sent the text to the owners. Within seconds, she had their reply. "They'll be back in fifteen minutes. They said the coffeepot's hot if we'd like to make ourselves a drink while we're waiting." Katie looked around the kitchen. Not only was the coffeepot hot, but the Princeton's had left four mugs and a plate of cookies sitting beside it. "Do you think they knew you'd want to live here?"

"Most people would want to live here. I owe your friend of a friend a big thank you."

"Shona will be happy knowing it's being rented by someone who appreciates the house."

"If the owners like me."

Katie poured two cups of coffee. "They'll like you. You ooze confidence and don't wear ripped jeans."

Peter looked at his trousers. "You don't like ripped jeans?"

"I don't mind what people wear, but Mr. and Mrs. Princeton are in their eighties. They'd wonder if you can afford the rent if you wore scruffy clothes."

Peter frowned and let her words settle in the silent room. "If I wasn't a chief executive, would it matter to you?"

Katie bit her bottom lip. "No. Did you think it would?"

He leaned against the counter. "People treat me differently when they know what I do and how much I earn. A few women I've dated expect a certain type of lifestyle when they're around me."

"Well, I'm not one of those people. I like to pay my own way wherever I go."

Peter stared at her for so long that she wondered what he

was thinking. So, instead of dwelling on his job, she changed the subject. "Charlie went ice skating this morning."

That made Peter's eyebrows rise. "Are you talking about Diana's dog or someone else?"

"Diana's dog. For most of the year, he loves jumping into the lake, but he usually stays away from the ice in the winter. But, for some reason, he ran onto the frozen lake this morning. He must have seen a rabbit or something. Diana thought he'd fall through the ice, but he came back."

"That must have given her a fright?"

"It did. She bought him a different harness so he doesn't run off like that again. Do you want to look in the garage while we're here?"

Peter sent her an amused smile. "I don't need to see it."

"Oh. What about the laundry and mudroom? They're important, especially in the winter."

"If they're anything like the rest of the house, they'll be more than okay. Just so you know, I earn more than six hundred thousand dollars a year. I reinvest most of that money into my company."

Katie choked on her drink.

Peter grabbed a paper towel off the counter and handed it to her. "Are you okay?"

"Not really." She gasped as her lungs started to breathe air instead of drowning in coffee. "That's a lot more than I earn waitressing."

Peter frowned. "With everything that's happening in the world, I feel like apologizing for earning that much money."

She blew her nose and hoped she hadn't made a complete fool of herself. "You work hard, just like everyone else. Besides, BioTech sponsors a lot of community programs."

"You know about them?"

For a moment, Katie wondered what she'd said wrong. Peter looked so shocked that she regretted saying anything.

"It's on your company's website. You gave away millions of dollars last year."

Peter sighed. "We did."

"You don't like talking about that, either?"

"It's not that. I'd asked Pastor—"

"Hello. We're home."

Katie dragged her gaze away from Peter and headed down the hallway. "We're in the kitchen, Mrs. Princeton."

Wrapped in a soft blue jacket and matching hat, Mrs. Princeton walked toward them. "It's so nice to see you again, Katie. And this must be your friend, Peter." She held out her hand. "My husband's parking our truck in the garage. It's lovely to meet you."

"It's nice to meet you, too." Peter shook her hand. "Your home is amazing."

"Thank you. I'll just take off my jacket and then you can tell me about yourself."

While she was in another room, hanging up her jacket, Katie grinned at Peter. "She likes you."

"How do you know?" he whispered.

"Female intuition."

"I hope you're right."

Katie knew she was. Especially when the chief executive of BioTech was pouring two more cups of coffee and moving them to the kitchen table. You'd have to be crazy not to see that this man, with all the weight of his company's future on his shoulders, wasn't the perfect person to rent this house. Or the perfect person to spend the rest of your life with.

CHAPTER 14

$\mathcal{A}$ week later, Barbara rushed into the kitchen at The Lakeside Inn. "Where's Diana and Penny?"

Katie looked up from the croissants she was baking. Her sister wasn't often flustered, but she was definitely worried about something. "Charlie was due for his vaccinations, so Diana drove him to the vet. Penny's working at the cottages on Anchor Lane. What's happened?"

"Chloe called. She's ninety-eight percent positive she knows where our great-grandfather's buried. The information they found has been verified as much as it can be."

Katie's eyes widened. "How did she find him?"

"A person on her team found a book about old cemeteries in Montana. She already knew Patrick died in a boating accident near Whitefish, so she looked at the cemeteries around that area. A man called Patrick James Kelly is buried in the Gregory Family Cemetery. It isn't far from Whitefish. There's something else you should know."

Katie wondered why her sister sounded so worried. Finding the grave was a fantastic discovery. It might give them more information about their great-grandfather and what had happened to him.

Barbara handed her a sheet of paper. "This was in the book. If the grave belongs to him, he was buried beside a woman and three children. They all had his last name."

Katie's eyes widened as she studied the picture. The second headstone belonged to a woman called Johanna Kelly. Buried with her were her children, Alice, Mary, and James. "They can't be his family. He was still married to Maggie when they died." She searched her sister's face, hoping she had more information about the people buried beside their great-grandfather.

"The Gregory family still owns the land the cemetery is on. Chloe's contacted them to see if they have any information about the people buried there. Johanna could be Patrick's brother's wife or a cousin, but we don't know if any of his siblings immigrated to America."

"Maggie never mentioned anything about her husband's family in her journals. I don't think Mom or Grandma ever said anything, either." Katie sat at the kitchen table before her legs gave way. Patrick James Kelly was always a shadowy figure in her grandmother's life. After he faked his death, he'd visited his family in Polson on more than one occasion. But, in all their research, no one had mentioned the possibility of him having another wife and children.

Taking a deep breath, she tried to think logically instead of assuming the worst. "We know Patrick worked on the steamboats and that he was a gambler. But that doesn't mean he married another woman when he was already married to Maggie. It might not even be his grave. There must have been a lot of men with his name who came to Montana from Ireland."

Barbara sat beside her. "He staged his own death to get

away from his gambling debts and gave his wife a letter written by Abraham Lincoln. Who knows what else he did?"

"Maggie loved him."

Barbara gave a resigned sigh. "I know, but would she still have loved him if he had another family?"

"I don't know." Their great-grandmother's life had been hard. There were many moments of sadness and despair in her journals; times when she didn't think she could support herself and her child. Imagining what Maggie would have done if Patrick had been unfaithful was foolish. She lived in a different time with issues Katie couldn't begin to understand. But if the grave beside Patrick's was his brother's wife and children, they could have more family living in Montana than they knew about.

Katie handed her sister the piece of paper. "Apart from contacting the Gregory family, is Chloe doing anything else to see if this Patrick Kelly is our great-grandfather and who the other people are?"

Barbara shook her head. "I don't think so. It could be a long wait to see if he's our great-grandfather."

Katie didn't want to wait that long. "The Smithsonian's getting ready for the opening of the exhibition about the letter. Chloe will appreciate having more information about the grave and the people buried there. Is the cemetery open to the public?"

"Don't even think about it," Barbara said quickly. "It's the middle of winter and the people buried in the graves might not be related to us."

With a determined glance at her sister, Katie pulled out her phone. "Someone named Patrick James Kelly was buried in the cemetery around the same time as Maggie received a condolence card from a friend. I want to see the grave."

"We already have a photo of the headstone. There isn't anything else to see."

"Beside from what the Gregory family has, there might be a chapel or some other records about the people buried in the cemetery."

Barbara frowned. "There's no point rushing off to Whitefish. Wait until Chloe calls us with more information."

"I'm not going there today."

Barbara breathed a sigh of relief. "Thank goodness for that. I thought…" She studied Katie's face. "When *are* you going?"

"Tomorrow. It will take me less than two hours to reach the cemetery."

"What if you can't drive onto the property?"

"Then I'll find someone in town who might know more about the graves. There must be a local history museum or an historical society in Whitefish." She showed her sister the map on her cell phone. "The property isn't far from town."

Barbara picked up the photo of the headstones. "I know why you want to do this, but it's winter. There's snow and ice everywhere, especially around the lake."

"I'll be careful."

"I've heard that before," she muttered. "You'd better pack a big picnic basket full of food."

"Why?"

"Because you aren't going there on your own. If you can take some time off work, so can I."

"You're coming with me?"

Barbara crossed her arms in front of her chest. "I think you're crazy but, yes, I'll go with you. At least if we get stuck in the snow, we can keep each other company."

Katie hugged Barbara tight. "You're the best sister in the world."

"That's what you say now. You might not like me so much if we get stranded in Whitefish. I'll remind you why we shouldn't have left Sapphire Bay."

"It won't be the first time you've told me what I should have done," Katie said with a grin.

"And it won't be the last. What time do you want to leave?"

Katie had seven guest breakfasts to prepare and a whole lot of other things to do before they left. "How about ten o'clock?"

"Ten sounds great. I'll meet you in the entryway. I have a few jobs I need to do in town before we leave."

With their plan firmly in place, Barbara left the kitchen and Katie returned to the counter. Sometimes, it seemed as though they were unraveling a ball of wool. Just when they thought they'd come to the end of their great-grandparent's story, a knot in the wool led to even more intrigue. Only this time, it could take them to places they'd never imagined their great-grandfather had gone. Especially if the family buried beside him were his second wife and children.

PETER UNDID HIS SEATBELT. Looking through the window, he stared at the heavy wooden gate separating Murray Ridge Road from the original Gregory family ranch. When Katie told him she was driving to Whitefish with her sister, he'd offered to come along. Other than the risk of having an accident, there was no way he wanted them meeting a stranger in the middle of a snow-covered ranch.

Katie flicked off her seatbelt. "Mr. Gregory said to open the gate and come up to the main homestead."

Peter stepped out of the truck. "I'll open it."

That didn't stop Katie from joining him. "I'll give you a hand."

There was no point arguing with her. She was one of the

most determined people he'd ever met. Holding her hand, he carefully stepped across the gravel driveway. "Are you still feeling excited about seeing the graves?"

"I was until Barbara stopped the truck. I always imagined our great-grandfather was like a modern-day Robin Hood. But instead of stealing from the rich, he beat them at poker and gave the money to his wife."

"If he was as successful as Robin Hood, he wouldn't have had to disappear."

"And my great-grandmother wouldn't have had to start her own business. Do you know how hard that must have been?"

Peter unclipped the heavy chain holding the gate and the fence posts together. "It would have been incredibly difficult. She couldn't go to the bank to borrow money and she probably didn't know anyone who could help finance what she needed. She would have had to build her business slowly and rely on word of mouth for advertising."

Pushing the gate wide, Katie waved her sister through. "Our great-grandmother was tough, stubborn, opinionated, and loved her daughter above everything else. Having to pretend her husband was dead must have gone against everything she believed in."

"She had the letter. Selling it would have solved all her problems."

Barbara drove the truck past them and stopped a few feet away.

"She must have realized how valuable it was."

Peter thought there was more to it than that. "Or she knew Abraham Lincoln's son would come looking for your great-grandfather if she sold it."

Katie stared at the steep, gabled roof of the house in the distance. "After everything they went through, the letter didn't make any difference to their lives. If Chloe's right, Patrick died in a boating accident not far from here and Maggie died alone in Polson. The person who lost the most was my grandma. She grew up without a father and her mom spent most of her time sewing other people's clothes to pay for food and rent."

"Was your grandma happy?"

Katie walked toward the truck. "It was all she knew, so I guess she was. Her happiest moments were with Granddad. When he died, it was like a light dimmed inside of her. She was still Grandma, but different."

Peter knew how that felt. When his grandmother died it took a long time for him to get used to her not being here. "Feeling that kind of loss makes you appreciate the people around you." He held Katie's hand, wanting her to know how special she was. "Whatever you discover today doesn't change who you are or how much your great-grandmother loved her husband. You have a loving family and lots of reasons to be happy."

The sadness in Katie's eyes disappeared. "And one of those reasons is you."

Before he could reply, Barbara rolled down the passenger window. "Come on you two, we have someone to meet and a cemetery to explore."

Peter kissed Katie lightly on the lips. "We'd better move. Barbara's not the most patient person I've met."

"I heard that," Barbara replied. "And just for the record, you're right."

With another look toward the Gregory family homestead, Peter opened Katie's door. Regardless of how many wives Patrick Kelly had, or what he'd done with his life, Peter was incredibly grateful Katie was here. She filled his world with laughter and happiness, and made him look forward to waking up each morning.

When she returned to Los Angeles, he didn't know what he'd do.

THE OLD METAL sign swinging from a rusty bracket sent a chill along Katie's spine. 'Lord remember me' wasn't the most inspiring words to see above the gate to the old cemetery, but it was probably fitting.

Steve Gregory, the great-great-grandson of the original settlers, must have seen her wary glance. "The words come from the gospel of Luke in the Bible. It's where the Good Thief, hanging on a cross beside Jesus, says, "Remember me when you come into your kingdom." I always thought it was fitting, considering a lot of my ancestors were cattle thieves and robbers."

Instead of making her feel less worried, Steve's explanation left her even more anxious. "Do you know why Patrick Kelly was buried here?"

The man who'd met them at the homestead rubbed the whiskers on his chin. "The best explanation I have is that he worked here. Only a few of the graves not belonging to my family have headstones. The others were marked by unnamed rocks."

Peter frowned. "He must have been highly regarded by your family."

"Or someone else paid for the headstone." Barbara turned to Katie. "Would our great-grandmother have paid for it?"

"If she'd known he'd died, she might have. But that doesn't account for the other headstone." Her hand tightened around Peter's. The family cemetery sat less than a thirty-minute walk from the original homestead. In the snow and ice, they'd made the journey on two of Steve's four-wheelers.

Tall trees surrounded three sides of the final resting place of the Gregory family. The fourth side overlooked pasture flattened by nature and now subdivided into large plots of land. Even from this distance, the houses looked much bigger than the homestead.

Steve walked through the ankle-deep snow to the far side of the fenced-off area. "My cousin wrote a book about the history of our family. I'll give you her cell phone number before you go. She might know something about your great-grandfather." He stopped in front of the same headstones Katie had seen in the photo. "This is what you've come to see."

Taking an old rag out of her pocket, Barbara knelt between the headstones. With gentle strokes, she wiped away the snow. When they could see the words, she pulled herself to her feet. "That's better."

Katie read the inscription on Patrick Kelly's headstone. 'Beloved husband and friend' only made her more confused. If her great-grandmother had paid for the headstone, wouldn't she have added her name and their daughter's?

Steve cleared his throat. "I'll check some fences while you're here. When do you think you'll be finished?"

Katie looked at Barbara and then at Peter. "In about fifteen minutes?"

Barbara stuck her hands in her jacket pockets. "Sounds good to me."

"I'll fit in with what you want to do," Peter added.

Steve nodded. "I'll be back soon. Feel free to look at the other graves."

After he'd gone, Katie sighed. "I expected to feel sad when I saw Patrick's headstone, but the only thing I feel is empty."

Barbara nodded. "It's hard to feel anything when we don't know if it's our great-grandfather's grave."

Peter studied the headstones. "The inscriptions don't tell us anything you didn't know before." Kneeling on the ground, he used his hands to scrape more snow from the base of Patrick's headstone. "When my grandmother died, Mom added a few words to the granite at the base of the headstone. I don't know whether anyone did the same—"

"Oh, my goodness," Barbara exclaimed as she peered over Peter's shoulders. "The snow's hiding some other words." Picking up the rag she'd left beside her, she handed it to Peter. "Use this. It might make it easier."

Katie moved closer. Her eyes widened when she saw the words 'm'anam, mo shaol'. "What does it mean?"

"I don't know." Barbara took her cell phone out of her pocket. "I installed an app a few months ago to translate some text for a client. All I have to do is type in the text and it'll tell me what language it is and what it means." After tapping in the phrase, she turned her phone around so Katie and Peter could see the translation. "It's Irish."

"My soul, my life," Katie murmured. "Whoever added it to the headstone must have loved him."

Barbara frowned. "I've heard the same words somewhere before. Does it mean anything to you, Katie?"

"Not that I remember."

Peter checked the base of Johanna's headstone, but there was nothing there. "I don't think you'll find any more clues here. We should check the other headstones to see who's buried in the cemetery."

Barbara wiped down the headstone beside Mary's. "The date they died might help us, too. Especially if we can read the book about the Gregory family history."

Katie solemnly looked at the other graves. "I feel like an intruder."

"The people buried here won't mind."

She glanced at Peter to see if he was joking. He wasn't. "I suppose you're right, but we'd better hurry. Steve will be back soon." Kneeling beside the grave closest to her, Katie used her gloves to carefully wipe the snow off the headstone. With Barbara taking photos of each grave, she gave the headstone belonging to Nellie Gregory an extra polish. Even though she'd died in 1902, Katie was sure she'd appreciate the gesture.

CHAPTER 15

*P*eter had never been to Whitefish, but driving past the historic red-brick and wooden buildings along Central Avenue reminded him of other small towns he'd visited in Montana.

"The library isn't far from here." Katie looked up from the map on her cell phone. "Take the next right, then turn left."

Fortunately, there wasn't much traffic on the road, so Barbara found the library without too much difficulty.

After they found a parking space, Katie slid her phone into her jacket pocket. "Whitefish always reminds me of a bigger version of Sapphire Bay."

"How many people live here?" Peter asked as he watched a family walk into the library.

Barbara opened the driver's door. "There are about eight thousand permanent residents, but the population doubles when everyone comes here to ski."

"It's a wonderful place to visit in the summer, too," Katie said. "Penny and Barbara have brought quite a few of our guests to Whitefish to enjoy the lake and the hiking trails."

"It sounds like I'll have to come back another time."

Katie pulled up the zipper on her jacket. "If you want company, I'll come with you. All I need is a few days' notice."

"You've got a deal." The grin she sent him made Peter's heart ache. He wanted to make the most of the time they still had together. May would come around far too quickly and, before he knew it, Katie would leave for Los Angeles.

"Thank goodness for snowplows," Barbara said as they made their way up the library steps. "This is a lot easier than visiting the cemetery."

"As long as we find more information than we did there, I'll be happy." Katie jogged ahead and opened the doors.

After they'd visited the cemetery, they'd looked online to see if there was a family history center in Whitefish. There wasn't, but most of the information they were looking for was available online. Instead of scrolling through their cell phones, they'd decided to visit the Whitefish Bay Public Library. That way, they could sit at different desks and check the birth, death, and marriage records on bigger screens.

"This is lovely," Katie said in a hushed voice as she stepped into the library.

Peter nodded his agreement. With its high cathedral ceiling and dark brown beams, it was the kind of cavernous room he could easily enjoy.

"Wait here," Barbara said as she studied the layout of the room. "I'll ask a librarian about their computers."

While she was gone, Peter followed Katie to some shelves filled with magazines.

"I wish our library had as many books and magazines as this one."

He frowned. "I didn't know Sapphire Bay had a library."

"It's only small, but it's great. Most of the books are donated by the community, so we have to wait to read the latest bestsellers."

Barbara came hurrying back. "We're in luck. There's a pod of three computers that haven't been booked. We can use them for the next hour."

Katie's hand wrapped around Peter's. "Are you ready to put your IT superpowers to good use?"

"Ready and willing, although it feels as though we're looking for a needle in a haystack."

"Or a man who didn't want to be found." Instead of looking depressed, Katie seemed excited. "Let's see how good my great-grandfather was at hiding."

For Katie and her family's sake, Peter hoped Patrick Kelly had underestimated how determined his family would be to find him—even if it was more than eighty years after he'd died.

KATIE SQUINTED as she scanned another set of marriage records. The quality of the entries had been getting progressively worse since she'd started looking for clues about her great-grandfather. "Is it me or are these records blurry?"

Barbara looked up from the computer she was using. "It's not your eyes. Someone's scanned the original records onto the database without editing the images."

"It was probably done like that because of the cost," Peter added. "I don't know how many years ago the records were scanned, but they wouldn't have had the same technology we do nowadays."

Rubbing her eyes didn't help, so Katie sat back in her chair and looked around the room. "At least it's warm and dry in the library."

"And there's a Starbucks and a bagel store not far from here." Barbara lifted her arms above her head and stretched. "We have ten minutes left of our allocated time. How about I buy everyone something to eat and drink after we've finished?"

"That sounds like bliss." Katie looked at the librarian sitting at the information desk. "Do you think we can reserve more time on the computers?"

"We could try. Do you need to be back in Sapphire Bay by a specific time, Peter?"

"I don't usually work on Saturdays and I didn't have anything else planned, so I can stay for as long as you like."

As she pushed her chair away from the desk, Katie glanced at the computer. "I'll ask if we can book another…" Leaning forward, she peered at the screen. Excitement buzzed inside her as she took a closer look at a marriage record. "I might have found something."

Barbara looked up from her computer. "What is it?"

"It's a marriage record for a man called John Kelly. He married Johanna Murphy in Havre, Montana on June 23, 1929. Didn't Chloe find a record of our great-grandfather staying in Havre in the 1920s?"

"I think so. Let me check." Picking up her phone, Barbara tapped on the screen. "I keep the spreadsheet of what we've discovered about Patrick on Dropbox. I'll open it and—"

Katie leaned over her sister's shoulder. "What does it say?"

Barbara enlarged the image. "You're right. Mr. and Mrs. P. Kelly checked into the Havre Hotel on June 21, 1929." Barbara's eyes widened. "Patrick must have been John Kelly's brother or maybe his cousin. He went to Havre for John's wedding."

Peter looked closely at the screen. "Click on the link. It should show us John and Johanna's marriage certificate."

Barbara opened the file and smiled. "Patrick James Kelly's listed as John's brother."

Katie sighed. "This is getting even more complicated. If

Johanna Kelly's buried with her children in the Gregory family cemetery, and Patrick was her brother-in-law, where's her husband?"

"We're looking for information about Patrick Kelly," Barbara said as she printed a copy of the marriage certificate. "As tempting as it is, we need to focus on that and not get sidetracked by looking at other relatives."

"But he could give us an insight into Patrick's life."

"He could also send us on a wild goose chase." Barbara added the copy of the certificate to the documents they'd brought with them. "We can research John Kelly another time."

Peter rubbed Katie's arm. "Does that make you feel better?"

"Not really, but Barbara's right. Hopefully, the book Steve Gregory's sending us will tell us why Patrick was in Whitefish."

Barbara pushed her chair away from the desk. "And after we've had something to eat and drink, we'll focus on finding our great-grandfather's death certificate."

Katie wasn't sure if they'd ever find an official record of his death. And maybe it didn't matter.

THE NEXT DAY, Katie handed Penny a large pry bar. "I can't believe how much information we found in the library. Even though they didn't have the original documents, they had databases filled with records about who lived in Whitefish in the 1900s as well as copies of the newspapers from around the area."

"It sounds like it was worthwhile going there. You might want to stand back."

Taking a few steps away from her sister, she watched in

awe as Penny hooked the end of the pry bar around some kitchen cabinets and ripped them from the wall. Katie jumped at the deafening thud of wood against wood.

The remodeling of the cottages Penny was working on wasn't supposed to start until next week. But, straight after Christmas, her impatient sister had decided to get a head start on the construction team.

Looking at what she'd achieved in such a short time, Katie couldn't help but feel proud of what Penny was doing. "I couldn't imagine this cottage being turned into a small business before you started, but now I can."

"Have a look at the plans. They're sitting on the table in the old living room."

Carefully, Katie made her way through the half-demolished wall separating the existing kitchen from the living areas. As she studied the architect's plans, she was even more impressed.

"This is the first time I've seen the drawings of what the outside of the building will look like. It will be gorgeous."

"I hope so. Can you give me a hand to get rid of these cabinets?"

Katie pulled on her leather gloves and walked back into the kitchen.

Penny was already holding one end of an old cabinet. With a lot of muscle and even more good luck, they carried it outside and threw it into the dumpster.

"One down, ten to go," Penny said with a grin.

"I can't believe you enjoy this so much."

"It's better than finding creative ways to sell another new multi-level building. Talking about changing careers, what are you doing here? I thought you'd be writing your next novel or spending time with Peter."

"I'm procrastinating."

Penny pointed to another cabinet. "Do you have writer's block?"

"No. I have boyfriend block." She placed her hands on either side of the cabinet and helped her sister lift it out of the kitchen. "Peter flew to New York City this morning. He wants to get a few things sorted before he moves here."

"And why do you have boyfriend block?"

Katie sighed. "I can't work out what to do next. I'll be going back to Los Angeles a few months after Peter comes back."

Penny lifted her end of the cabinet higher as they slowly made their way down the porch steps. "If that's a problem, why don't you stay here?"

"Because I live in Los Angeles. My friends are there. My agent—"

"I get it. She lives there, too. But why do you have to stay there? You enjoy cooking the meals for our guests and helping us with the other things we need. You've even said writing is easier from Sapphire Bay."

Katie stopped in front of the dumpster. "What if I stay here and my relationship with Peter fizzles out to nothing? I would have given up my life in Los Angeles for a broken heart."

"At least you'd know Peter wasn't meant to be. On the count of three, we'll lift the cabinet and throw it into the dumpster. Are you ready?"

After repositioning her hands, Katie nodded.

"One, two, *three*."

With more muscle power than she thought she had, Katie hoisted the cabinet into the air. The satisfying clunk as it hit something else made her smile. "How do you do this each day? My arms feel like they're about to fall off."

"You get used to it. It wasn't until after we worked on the

inn that I realized how strong I'd become. And, by the way, there's nothing wrong with having your heart broken. It means you've trusted someone enough to make them matter to you. That's not a bad thing."

"It is if you prefer to live a happy life."

Penny stuck her hands on her hips. "Can you honestly tell me your life will be happy without Peter?"

"I was happy before I met him," Katie said stubbornly.

"No, you weren't. You were miserable. When you weren't working at the restaurant or writing, you spent most of your time complaining about not having a publishing contract. Now look at you. You've published your first six children's books and lots of people have bought them. That's a whole lot of reasons why moving back to Sapphire Bay was the best thing you've ever done."

Katie looked at the truck pulling into the driveway and waved at Wyatt. "Moving home was the best thing that's happened to you, too."

The look that Penny sent her was bittersweet. "Don't be fooled by what you see now. I had my fair share of boyfriend block, too, but everything worked out in the end."

"Well, whatever you did to fix it was worth it." With one last look at the cottage, Katie handed her gloves to Penny. "Thanks for listening to me. I'd better go home and do some more writing."

"Good luck. Diana called me an hour ago and said the water pipes are making a strange gurgling noise. The plumber should be there sometime this afternoon."

"As long as the pipes don't explode, we'll be fine." At least, she hoped they were. "Are you and Wyatt coming to the inn for dinner tonight?"

"We wouldn't miss it for the world. It isn't often we have a barbecue in the middle of winter."

Katie smiled. "It's Dad's way of living dangerously. See you later." As she made her way out to her truck, she thought about Peter. He was changing his life around to spend more time with her. If he was so sure about his feelings, why was she holding back so much?

CHAPTER 16

*A*cid burned in Peter's stomach as he listened to David O'Dowd, his clinical director, tell him the results of their investigation into the stolen report.

"The intern position has been terminated and we're reviewing our policy around hiring college graduates." David handed him a folder. "This is the assessment the security team completed. The good news is that they didn't identify any other potential security breaches."

"What's the bad news?"

"That we had to do it in the first place. The person responsible for leaking the report passed the police and credit check. There was absolutely nothing in their application form to suggest they would be susceptible to bribes. Even their colleagues were shocked they'd stolen information that was supposed to be confidential."

"We can't afford to make the same mistake again."

David nodded. "We'll do everything we can to make our processes watertight. But I can't guarantee no one will ever be able to do the same thing again. We can have all the security features available to mankind, but if someone's intent on stealing information, it's impossible to stop them."

David was right, but that didn't make any difference to how Peter felt when he thought about the person who'd stolen the report.

"On a brighter note, we had extremely positive results from the new coding we added to the prosthetic software. It's making even the smallest movement more precise for our clients." David referred to the notes on his phone. "All trial participants have uploaded the enhancement and ninety-two percent noticed a significant improvement in their mobility."

Peter refocused his brain. If he dwelled on what had happened with the stolen report, he wouldn't make the most of being here. "That's fantastic. Email me the details and I'll add them to the presentation I'm making to some potential funders."

"You'll have them shortly after our meeting. Are you sure you want to go back to Montana? This is a crucial time for the next phase of the project."

"I'll still work from New York City for three days every couple of weeks. When I'm not here, I'll be available by phone, email, and through teleconferencing meetings."

David didn't look convinced that working from Sapphire Bay was a good idea.

"If it doesn't work, I can easily come back here."

"Would your girlfriend be happy if you moved back to New York City?"

"Neither of us may have a choice." Peter didn't want to consider what would happen if his team needed him here. With Katie leaving for Los Angeles in May, it would be a hard time for both of them.

David studied his face. "The scholarships you want BioTech to sponsor are ready to go."

"Thanks for speaking to the finance team. I know how busy you are."

"If you're happy, I'm happy. Now, if you'll excuse me, I need to get ready for another meeting. Good luck with the charity dinner tonight."

Peter sent his friend a wry grin. "I'm only going because two of our major sponsors will be there."

"You'll still need luck. From what I've heard, Ian Galloway's redirecting a lot of his philanthropic funding toward the library at Yale."

"If that's what he chooses to do, I can't change his mind."

David stood. "Read the testimonials from our trial participants. Their stories might be enough to sway Ian. And don't beat yourself up about not being here. As much as it hurts me to say it, no one's indispensable."

"Not even the person who started the company?"

"You've created an outstanding team who would walk over hot coals for you. If you want to divide your time between Montana and New York, we'll do everything we can to make it work. If it doesn't, we'll tell you."

Peter hoped they did because, right at this moment, he felt like a human rubber band. Unfortunately, there was only so much stretching you could do before something snapped. And, with how he was feeling, that could happen anytime soon.

KATIE YAWNED as Barbara explained how to create a Facebook ad. "I'm sorry. I've had a few late nights and I'm exhausted."

"I thought I was boring you to death."

"It's not that it's boring. It's just not the type of thing I enjoy."

"Which is why I created another series of ads for you. The first ones we uploaded have done extremely well." Barbara frowned. "Have you heard from Peter since he left?"

"He calls me each night."

"How does he feel about being back in New York?"

Katie leaned her elbows on the desk and sighed. "He's enjoying it but he's busy. Most nights this week he's either been meeting people who can fund the next phase of his project or visiting his family. They like having him home."

"From what he said, they're a close family."

"They are. His brother and sister haven't stopped calling him a cowboy since he told them he's moving to Montana. His parents have already planned a trip to Sapphire Bay next month."

Barbara opened another document on her computer. "It's just as well he has plenty of spare rooms in the house he's rented. It must have been a big decision for him."

"Deciding to live in Sapphire Bay?"

"That and starting a relationship with you."

Katie's eyes widened. Her sister couldn't mean what Katie thought she did. "What do you mean?"

"You don't have a great track record when it comes to men."

Even though it was true, Katie was annoyed her sister thought it was relevant to her relationship with Peter. "I had to focus on work, not my personal life. Otherwise, I'd be another homeless statistic in Los Angeles."

"Peter's staying here to spend more time with you, but you're still moving back to California."

"I'm going because I need to live there."

"No. You're going because you're running away again."

Katie's heart pounded. "I've never run away from anything—"

"From the time you were ten years old, you wanted to

leave Sapphire Bay. What we have here was never enough for you."

Of all the things her sister could have said, that upset Katie the most. "I can't believe you said that. It was all very well for you and Penny. You have incredible careers with clients all around America. Did you ever think that maybe your success was a little intimidating? That I needed to move to Los Angeles to give myself the best chance of becoming as successful as you are?"

"Don't be silly. We've worked hard for what we have—"

"And you think I haven't?" Katie's voice cracked with emotion as every insecurity she'd buried came rushing to the surface. "I've had to work more hours than you do just to pay my rent. On a good day, I earn more in tips than I do in wages. Every single day is a struggle. When I write, I'm not earning any money, but I have to write if I want to publish more books."

"If you stay in Sapphire Bay, you could live here, cook for our guests, and not worry about running out of money. You'd have a comfortable life that lets you focus on your writing career."

Katie threw her hands in the air. "I don't want to be comfortable. I want to have an exciting, action-packed life. I want to travel and meet different people, and write stories that make a difference in children's lives."

Barbara crossed her arms in front of her chest. "You'll be thirty years old next year. It's time you realized that life isn't one big adventure, especially when your boyfriend is the chief executive of a company. He has responsibilities, people who depend on him."

"What do you think is keeping me awake at night? I know he has responsibilities. He's doing important work and changing people's lives. And what am I doing? Cooking for our guests and writing children's stories in my spare time. I'll never be able to write full time."

"Now you've reduced your life to a pity party."

Katie took a deep breath. "Is this pick-on-Katie week? Penny told me I'm crazy to think about going back to Los Angeles. Now you're telling me I'm crazy no matter what I do."

Diana hurried into the office. "Keep your voices down. Our guests have just come back from Wild Horse Island and they don't need to hear your argument."

"We aren't arguing," Barbara said in a hushed whisper. "I'm trying to make Katie see how short-sighted she's being."

"I'm not short-sighted," Katie hissed. "I'm careful."

Diana glared at both of them. "Well, whatever you are, have your discussion outside. Preferably on the far side of the lake and away from everyone else."

Katie picked up the spreadsheet Barbara had given her. "We don't need to go anywhere. Our discussion is over."

Barbara sighed. "Not quite. I have some news about the inscription on Patrick's headstone."

Charlie wandered into the office and Diana patted his back. "Did you find something in our great-grandmother's journals?"

Katie's eyebrows rose. "You didn't tell me you were looking through them. If I'd known, I could have helped."

"It wasn't a big deal. Theo's doing research for another article, so I had some spare time. The reason I thought I recognized the words was because they're in one of Maggie's journals. I'll show you." Barbara opened a folder on her computer.

Katie looked at the screen. Chloe's team at the Smithsonian had sent them paper and digital copies of their great-grandmother's journals. That way, the originals would be safe with the museum, and Katie's family could still read them.

Barbara scrolled through the earliest journal they'd found. "Here it is." Pointing to the image, she read the words, "M'anam, mo shaol. My soul, my life. They were part of Maggie and Patrick's wedding vows. The man buried in the cemetery at Whitefish must be our great-grandfather."

Diana leaned against the doorframe. "That's romantic and sad at the same time. Imagine loving someone so much and only being able to see them every now and then. It would have been heartbreaking."

"I wonder why Maggie didn't move to Whitefish to live with her husband?" Katie asked.

"She must have been worried someone would find them."

"Don't forget she was running a successful sewing business in Polson," Barbara added. "If she'd moved, she wouldn't have had that income."

"They were stuck living separate lives."

Katie didn't know if Maggie would have seen it that way. From what she'd said in her journals, she loved her husband dearly, but worried about his gambling addiction. She had a thriving business, a daughter she adored, and good friends who cared about her. Giving up that kind of security to live with a man who wasn't the most reliable person in the world would be hard for anyone.

With a grimace, she realized she was beginning to think like Barbara. "Patrick might not have been as bad as we think he was. If his brother had died or abandoned his wife and children, Patrick might have been in Whitefish looking after them."

Barbara sat back in her chair. "But did he do it out of a sense of obligation or guilt?"

Katie frowned. Trust Barbara to look for the negatives. "Does it make any difference?"

"It did to Maggie and our grandma. From what we've discovered, they hardly saw him."

Diana sighed. "Grandma was the most forgiving person I know. Regardless of what her father was like, she loved him. I never heard her say one unkind thing about her dad."

Katie glanced at Barbara, hoping her opinion of Patrick softened. "It was a different time. We only have our great-grandmother's journals to know what their lives were like and, from what we've read, they weren't easy."

"No one's lives were easy then." Barbara rubbed her forehead. "I'm sorry for what I said about Peter and staying here. Whatever you decide to do, we'll understand and support you."

Diana nodded. "And whether you write more books or not, we'll still love you."

With a heavy heart, Katie looked at the spreadsheet she was holding. After talking about Peter and moving back to Los Angeles, the marketing plan for her books didn't seem nearly as important as it was an hour ago.

PETER CLOSED the door to his office in New York City and sighed. After spending two weeks here, he couldn't wait to return to Sapphire Bay.

A year ago, he would have told anyone he enjoyed his job. Developing high-tech solutions to everyday problems made the long hours he worked worthwhile.

Meeting with suppliers, funding agencies, and the technical teams he employed made each day different. He thrived on a challenge, and BioTech certainly had a lot of those.

But, after working from Sapphire Bay, he craved the peace and tranquility that came with living in a small town. He even missed seeing Mabel and Allan in the general store and walking into Sweet Treats to sample Brooke's latest batch of fudge.

When he'd told his colleagues about Sapphire Bay, he thought they'd think he was mad to want to leave the bright lights of New York City behind. Surprisingly, the complete opposite had happened.

Before they joined his team, two of the IT specialists working on the prosthetic project had worked in Bozeman with a tech start-up company. They hadn't been to Sapphire Bay, but they'd traveled around Flathead Lake, stopping at Polson, Whitefish, and Bigfork. When he'd half-jokingly mentioned opening an offsite lab in Sapphire Bay, they'd jumped at the chance of relocating to Montana. Even David, his clinical director, had asked probing questions about the price of houses and the quality of the coffee.

A few days later, more staff stopped him in the corridors and in the cafeteria. They asked if he was serious about setting up another office in Montana. If the gossip mill went any faster, half his staff would be packing their bags and coming back with him.

Walking across to his office window, he stared at the streetlights far below. He could imagine the sound of taxi horns honking as they lined up like Formula One drivers at the traffic lights, the toxic smell of exhaust fumes, and the window displays from the stores dotted along the street.

Right now, he'd give anything to be sitting in front of the huge fireplace at The Lakeside Inn sipping coffee, and listening to Katie tell him about her latest book. Just thinking about being there made him homesick—and that was something he hadn't felt in years.

A soft tap on his door made him turn around. "Come in."

David stepped into the room. "I saw your lights were still on. How was the meeting with the Galloway Trust?"

"Better than I expected. Ian had a lot of questions but

seemed happy with my answers. He's given me his verbal agreement to fund stage two of the project. His legal team will draw up the funding contract in the next few days."

David tilted his head to the side. "That must be a relief?"

"It is."

"It doesn't sound like it. The Peter Bennett who started this company would have been buzzing with excitement if he'd had that type of news."

"That was a few years ago."

"I keep forgetting you were a child protégé. Even thirty-six-year-old men are allowed to get excited about a multimillion-dollar funding package. Especially when it'll change people's lives."

"I am excited." Peter forced a smile. "See. This is my happy face."

David's eyes narrowed. "What's wrong?"

"You'll think I'm crazy if I tell you."

"Is this about your grand plan to open another office in Sapphire Bay?"

Peter sat heavily in his office chair. "It's more than that. When I'm not here, I miss my family and working alongside you and the rest of our team. But I don't miss Manhattan. I think I'm going through a mid-life crisis."

"Or a re-evaluation of what's important. You've found someone special in Sapphire Bay. Don't give up on her."

"Are those wise words coming from personal experience?" Peter only knew the bare facts about David's last girlfriend, but even that was enough to make him want to take the next flight back to Montana.

"Chrissy and I had a great relationship. I enjoy my job, but leaving her was the worst thing I ever did."

"Have you called her to tell her that?"

"There's no point. She's engaged to someone else." David sat in the chair opposite him. "I'm forty years old with no wife, no children, and a mortgage that makes my eyes water. I have a great job, good friends, and a sweet tooth that constantly leads me astray. If I were in your shoes, I'd be setting up an office in Sapphire Bay, too."

"Katie wants to live in Los Angeles. By the time everything's organized, she'll be gone."

"Maybe. Maybe not. If you can negotiate a multimillion-dollar funding deal, you can convince her to stay in Montana. Or come here. Or help you find a building big enough for half your staff in Los Angeles."

"You make it sound so simple."

"It is, if you want it to be." David picked up his backpack. "I'm heading home to console myself with a tub of ice cream. Do you want to join me?"

Peter looked at the stack of folders on his desk. There was nothing that couldn't wait until tomorrow. "Are you still obsessed with buttered pecan?"

"I've moved on to cookies and cream."

"In that case, I'm in." Pushing his future to one side, Peter followed David out of the office. If his friend could find comfort in ice cream, there was hope for him, too.

CHAPTER 17

atie checked her watch for the tenth time in as many minutes. Peter should have arrived hours ago. But, after flying into the airport at Kalispell, he'd been held up behind an accident somewhere between Elmo and Sapphire Bay. To stop herself from getting too anxious, she'd offered to help her parents in the general store.

"Take this box of fabric across to the quilting area before you wear a hole in the floorboards," Mabel said. "Peter will be here as soon as he can."

Taking the cardboard box out of her mom's hands, she maneuvered around their customers. The quilting table was full of fabric swatches in all colors of the rainbow. Taking pride of place behind the fabric was the sewing machine that had arrived before Christmas. She was surprised it was still here.

The bell above the door jingled, but she didn't pay it any attention. With all the ski slopes closed because of the weather, many of the tourists who'd traveled to Montana were exploring the towns around Flathead Lake.

Opening the box, she sorted the fabric squares into colors

and carefully laid them on the table. Anyone who enjoyed quilting would be excited to see the gorgeous fabric.

"That's my favorite." Mabel pointed to a rich, ruby red fabric with tiny yellow bumblebees on it. "It reminds me of the beehives your granddad used to have. There was nothing he liked better than spending time with his bees."

"His neighbors enjoyed the hives as well," Katie said. "Especially after Granddad harvested the honey. He was a talented man."

Mabel nodded. "He would often stare across the lake from his rocking chair and tell me this was his little patch of heaven. It only seems like yesterday he was in the garden, pruning Grandma's roses."

Katie remembered talking around the dinner table about the new varieties of roses and which ones her grandma wanted him to grow next. "He loved making Grandma happy."

"She felt the same way about him." Reaching into the box, Mabel placed half a dozen blue fabric squares beside the purple ones. "Barbara said you still want to move back to Los Angeles. I thought you and Peter were getting along really well."

"We are, but I need to be where the editors and publishing houses are based."

"Wouldn't New York City be better? Not that I want you to move there, but it makes more sense for your writing career."

"All the publishing houses I want to work with have offices in California. My agent lives in Los Angeles and, out of the two options, she thought I'd have more chance of being picked up by a publishing house if I lived in California." Katie looked down at her cell phone. "I'll just get this call."

"Is it Peter?"

Katie shook her head. "It's my agent," she whispered before saying, "Hi, Nalini. How are you?"

"Better than I was last week. How's Montana?"

"Cold, dark, and filled with the smell of hot chocolate and marshmallows."

"Spoken like a true country girl. I have some good news."

Katie sighed. "Brad Pitt just walked into your office and wants to buy the film rights to my books?"

"Not quite, but close. I just heard from the editor at Plumridge Books. They want to talk to you about writing a new series of children's books."

"Are you serious?" On Katie's list of most preferred publishing houses, Plumridge Books was at the top. Her agent had sent her manuscripts to them and each time they'd been declined.

"I'm as serious as you are about hot chocolate. The editor's daughter was reading one of your books and loved it. After her mom read it, she bought the rest of the series and called me."

"Why didn't they want the manuscripts when we first approached them?"

"They've had a change of staff and focus. They like the way you mix genres and create a world that resonates with children. Anything that combines magic and adventure themes is flying off the shelves. There's something else they want you to consider. I'll email you the details."

Katie glanced at her mom. Mabel had finished laying the quilting fabric on the table and was looking excitedly at her. "When do they want to talk to me?"

"As soon as you can organize a flight to Los Angeles."

With a pounding heart, Katie smiled at her mom. "I'll check the flights and call you with some options."

"Sounds great. If I don't answer my work number, call me on my cell phone. Congratulations!"

"Thanks, Nalini. I'll be in touch soon." After she ended the call, Katie's eyes filled with tears. "Plumridge Books wants to talk to me about writing a series of books for them."

"That's fantastic. I'm so happy for you."

Katie's hand was trembling so much she almost dropped her phone. "I don't want to get my hopes up. It's only the first conversation. They might not want to go ahead after we talk."

"Nonsense. They'd be crazy not to sign you up, then and there." Mabel hugged Katie tight. "It's everything you've ever wanted."

Katie's smile disappeared. It wasn't everything, but it was close.

PETER PULLED himself out of his truck and took a deep, cleansing breath. With snow causing havoc on the roads, the usual hour it took to travel from Kalispell Airport to Sapphire Bay had taken four. Regardless of the slow drive, it felt good to finally be back.

He could have stood on the sidewalk for a lot longer, enjoying the view of the quaint stores and snow-capped mountains, but he'd sooner find Katie, wrap her in his arms, and tell her how much he'd missed her.

"Peter! When did you get home?" Penny stepped onto the sidewalk holding a reciprocating saw.

"I just drove into Sapphire Bay. What are you doing with the saw?"

"The blade's bent and I need to buy a new one. Dad said he had some spares in the general store, so that's where I'm heading."

"Katie said I'd find her in the general store, too. I'll walk with you. How's the remodeling of the cottages going?"

"Really well. The construction team's amazing and the plumbers and electricians start work tomorrow. We're trying not to get too far ahead of ourselves in case we have a problem sourcing building supplies."

"That makes sense. Ethan was looking for some reclaimed wood for one of his projects and couldn't find any. There seems to be a shortage of everything at the moment." Peter stopped in front of the general store. "It's good to be home."

"Katie will like that you said Sapphire Bay feels like home." Penny opened the door. "Hopefully, it still feels like home to her, too."

Peter frowned. "What do you mean?"

With a shrug that didn't seem as relaxed as it should have, Penny stepped inside the store. "Sometimes, you need to be reminded about what's really important."

"Someone I know said the same thing."

Penny held the saw higher. "I'll find dad and get some blades. Good luck with Katie."

He didn't know why Penny thought he would need luck, but he'd take what he could get. After two weeks away, he'd realized fairly quickly that he didn't like long-distance relationships.

Mabel hurried across the store. "My two favorite people," she gushed. "Katie said you were held up on the road, Peter. You must be exhausted."

"It wasn't too bad. The accidents I saw didn't look too serious."

"I'm glad. Being told a loved one has been involved in an accident is the last thing anyone wants to hear. Would you like a cup of coffee?"

He shook his head, not wanting to be a bother. "I'm okay, but thanks for the offer."

"Katie's in the workroom. Go on through."

As he walked toward the back of the store, he looked at

the changes Mabel had made since he was last here. It was nothing short of a miracle. Instead of tinsel and decorations strung around the store, everything was as neat as a pin and looked anything other than Christmassy.

It never failed to amaze him how quickly each year went by. Twelve months ago, his company was about to trial the third prototype of the neural gel prosthetics. Everyone was excited about the enhancements and were looking forward to seeing just how much of a difference they made. Now, here he was, about to sign a multimillion-dollar contract to produce custom-made prosthetics that would transform thousands of people's lives.

He opened the workroom door and smiled at Katie. She was standing on a three-step ladder, counting the boxes on a shelf. "Hello, stranger."

The clipboard she was holding clattered against the shelf. Seconds later, a huge smile lit her face. "You're here!"

Peter laughed as she jumped off the ladder and rushed toward him. The hug she wrapped him in was every bit as exuberant as it always was. "I've missed you."

"I missed you, too. What are you doing?"

"I'm helping Dad with this year's inventory. How are you feeling?"

"Tired, but it's good to be back. I bought you a present."

Katie frowned. "You didn't have to do that."

"Yes, I did." Reaching into his jacket pocket, he took out a small gift-wrapped package. "I saw it in a store in Brooklyn."

With more care than usual, Katie undid the ribbon and peeled back the wrapping paper. The silver key chain sparkled in the overhead fluorescent lights.

With a sigh, she read the engraved message. *"Take pride in how far you've come. Have faith in how far you can go. But don't forget to enjoy the journey.* That's so lovely. Thank you."

"You're welcome. I thought it was an important message to remember."

"It is."

Her softly spoken words worried him. "What's wrong?"

Before she was able to tell him, Mabel opened the work-room door and hurried toward them. "Allan's looking after the front counter, so I don't have a lot of time. Have you told Peter about the contract you've been offered?"

Katie's face turned bright red. "Not yet."

"I thought it would have been the first thing you told him." Mabel turned to Peter. "It's so exciting. I've told all my friends and they are so impressed. And it was all because you gave Katie the push she needed to self-publish her books. We can't thank you enough."

The door into the workroom opened and Allan poked his head around the doorframe. "I need you out here, Mabel. Hi, Peter. Welcome back."

"Thanks."

Mabel sent Peter a beaming smile. "We've all missed you. If you'd like to come to dinner tomorrow night, you're more than welcome. Ethan and Theo will be there with Diana and Barbara."

Peter glanced at Katie before replying. She looked so uncomfortable that he wasn't sure if it was a good idea. "Thanks for the invitation. Can I let you know later tonight if I can make it? Zac mentioned something about tomorrow night, too."

"That's no problem. If you're busy tomorrow, then anytime's fine." With a cheerful wave, Mabel rushed back into the front of the store.

The silence filling the workroom was more over-whelming than Mabel's greeting.

Katie clutched the keyring in her hand. "My agent called me."

"What did she say?"

"She wants me to fly to Los Angeles and speak to one of the biggest children's publishing houses in the country. The acquiring editor of Plumridge Books read my stories and loved them." Taking a deep breath, she continued, "They want me to write a new series of stories for them."

A glimmer of hope made Peter's heart pound. If Katie was offered a contract, she wouldn't have to live in Los Angeles, chasing a dream that had already happened. But, considering how stressed she looked, there had to be more to the offer.

"That's great news, isn't it?"

"It is." Clasping her hands in front of her, she took a deep breath. "Plumridge Books is sponsoring a six-month Writers in Residence Program at UCLA for emerging authors. As well as writing the new series, they want me to be the first children's author to participate in the program. It's a huge honor."

His hopes plummeted. It was hard enough being separated from Katie for two weeks. Six months would be horrendous. "When does it start?"

"At the beginning of their spring quarter. I'd need to be living in the apartment they provide by mid-March."

"That's only four weeks away."

"It's a few months earlier than I thought I'd be leaving. I'm not even sure it'll be possible. I'll have to ask Grandma's lawyer if I can leave before the twelve-month term in her will is over."

The sharp sting of disappointment hit him in the chest. Not once had she mentioned their relationship. "Do you want to go to UCLA?"

"That's where I completed my degree, so I know the campus and how everything works. The staff are wonderful and it would give me plenty of time to write without having to waitress at the restaurant."

"It sounds like you're looking forward to it."

Katie's eyes misted over. "It's a once-in-a-lifetime opportunity."

"So are we."

"It doesn't have to be the end. If I accept the position, we could still keep in contact. It's only for six months. After that—"

"After that I'll be in New York City. You don't want to live there, so we'll be back to living more than two thousand miles apart." He focused on the wall behind her instead of the pleading look in her eyes. "I understand why you want to go. I hope everything works out with your grandma's lawyer."

And before she saw just how upset he was, he left the workroom and strode toward the front of the store. He needed to get out of here before Mabel and Allan saw him. It was bad enough seeing the disappointment on Katie's face without dealing with her parents' reaction.

With a sinking heart he thought about the next six months. If Katie left, there wasn't much point thinking they could build a life together. It would be better to make a clean break and give them both a chance to focus on the future.

A future that seemed even more bleak than it was before he'd left for New York.

THREE DAYS LATER, Katie sat in her truck, staring at the gorgeous house Peter was moving into. Cherry Blossom Lane sat like a majestic jewel in the streets around it. Usually, when she saw the white picket fences and wraparound porches, she imagined the wonderful moments the people living there must have. But nothing about today's visit would be wonderful.

She'd spoken to Nicola Lassiter, the acquiring editor at

Plumridge Books. She seemed like a bright and bubbly person. The kind of person she'd enjoy working with. In four days, Katie would fly to Los Angeles, meet the wider publishing team, and visit the UCLA campus where she'd spend six months writing and lecturing.

If she signed the contract.

Diana and Penny thought she was crazy to even consider not working with Nicola and her team. Barbara hadn't said much, but Katie knew she wanted her to stay in Sapphire Bay. Her grandma's lawyer still hadn't told her whether she could work in Los Angeles a few weeks earlier than planned, but it seemed unlikely he'd say no.

Now, here she was, about to ask Peter to give their relationship another chance.

She jumped when someone tapped on the driver's window.

"Are you going to sit inside your truck all day?" Zac asked. "We'd appreciate having another pair of hands to help move everything inside."

With a decisive nod, Katie grabbed her bag and the box of muffins she'd made this morning. It was time to tell Peter when she was going to Los Angeles for the meeting. And if she planned on staying there.

CHAPTER 18

*P*eter was walking upstairs with two suitcases when the front door opened. Zac had left a few minutes ago to bring some boxes inside, so he assumed it was him.

"You can leave the boxes beside the closet in the hall," he said over his shoulder.

"I don't have your towels and sheets," Zac said. "But I do have a box that smells like cinnamon and lemon."

What on earth was Zac talking about? Peter turned around. "I don't have anything..." His voice dropped to a whisper. Katie stood in the entryway in front of Zac. Her red curls were pushed under a black wooly hat and she looked pale and drawn. Two words he never thought he'd use to describe her.

"I baked fresh muffins this morning," she said with a shy smile. "I thought you might enjoy them after you've moved everything inside."

A longing that went deeper than anything he'd ever known blocked Peter's throat. With more effort than Katie would ever realize, he opened his mouth to speak. "Thanks."

Zac looked at Peter as if he was waiting for him to say something else. What could he say that hadn't been said? Katie was leaving. Not out of necessity or because she had some life-threatening reason to move. She wanted to work from Los Angeles. And after her six-month residency was over, she'd probably stay.

Zac left the muffins on the hall table. "If you'd like to join us for coffee, Katie, we shouldn't be too much longer."

Peter's gaze shot to his friend. How could he invite her to stay when he knew they hadn't spoken to each other for three days? With a lift to his chin, Zac sent him a look that told him to grow up. So much for their friendship.

The silence inside the house was deafening.

"I'll bring the other boxes inside." Zac's voice broke the tension sneaking up Peter's spine. "Remember to plug in the coffeepot. I'll have a drink, too."

After he disappeared outside, Katie lifted her gaze to where Peter stood on the stairs. "Penny told me you were moving in today. How's it going?"

"It's taking a lot less time than I thought." After leaving the suitcases on the landing, he walked downstairs. The longing that had overwhelmed him receded to a dull ache. "I only had a few suitcases and some boxes to move. Most of the things I sent from New York haven't arrived."

"You should have called me. I could have helped."

That would have opened a wound that was already raw. "Barbara said you're busy at the inn. I didn't want to bother you."

"It would have been all right. Four of our guests left yesterday and another six people arrived this morning. Everyone's going out for dinner, so I don't need to bake anything until tomorrow." She looked around the entryway and frowned. "This looks different."

"The owners put a lot of their smaller ornaments and

furniture into storage. Without the extra pieces, it makes everything look a lot bigger."

"And less cluttered." Katie's gaze settled on two stacked boxes. He'd bought the cookware sets from her parents at the general store. "Are they pots and pans or is there something else inside?"

"They're pots and pans." When she lifted her eyebrows, a smile pulled at the corners of his mouth. "I prefer to use my own kitchen things when I'm staying somewhere for a few months."

"I can understand that. I'd hate to bake with someone else's things, too. I'm glad you're staying in Sapphire Bay. I thought you might have changed your mind after...after everything that's happened." She picked up one of the boxes. "I'll take this into the kitchen."

"Be careful. It's heavier than it looks."

Katie rebalanced the box in her arms. "It's all right. I've carried heavier ones."

Peter picked up the other box and followed her down the hallway. "I've enjoyed living in Montana, so I'll stay. If anything, it'll be good for my senior team to get used to me not being in the office all the time. What have you been doing?"

"I've written another chapter in my book, scheduled some Facebook ads, and bought Charlie a birthday present. He'll be ten years old next week."

Stepping around her, he held open the kitchen door. "He doesn't look that old."

"He gets pampered more than the average dog." Carefully, she slid the heavy box onto the kitchen counter. "I still can't believe you'll be living here."

"Neither can I. I'm grateful you recommended me to your friend."

"I guess it was meant to be."

He glanced at Katie before leaving his box beside hers. With everything inside of him, he wished a lot of other things were meant to be. "When are you leaving for the meeting in Los Angeles?"

"On Thursday morning."

"That's tomorrow."

"It was the only available seat I could find. A lot of people must be escaping the cold to go to California."

Peter frowned. "Is someone picking you up from the airport?"

"Nalini, my agent, will be waiting for me. I'll spend the night at her apartment before meeting the team from Plumridge Books. After I've spoken to them, I'll head out to UCLA to look at the art department and the accommodation they're offering. I'm flying home on Saturday."

He wouldn't ask her if she was signing the contract—he already knew the answer. "You have a full schedule."

Katie walked across to a wall of cupboards and opened the doors. "I wanted to make the most of my time while I was there. I haven't been back to Los Angeles since Grandma died." Taking three mugs out of the cupboard, she turned to Peter. "I still haven't made up my mind about the Writers in Residence Program."

"But you want to live in Los Angeles?"

"I think so."

Peter swallowed the fear rising inside of him. If he didn't tell Katie how he felt about her, it could be too late by the weekend. "I think I'm falling in love you, Katie. Whatever decision you make about living in Los Angeles is up to you, but long-distance relationships never work. I missed you while I was in New York and I can't imagine spending six months away from you."

"I missed you, too. Even if I'm living in Los Angeles, we could make it work. We could—"

"I can't do it, Katie. If I didn't have a business to run, I'd move to the end of the world for you. But I can't afford to open an office in Los Angeles."

"I never expected you would."

Peter ran his hand through his hair. He'd always been in control of his own destiny, always searching for ways to make life better for him and the people he cared about. But, this time, all he had was complete and utter honesty to try to make Katie see how much she meant to him.

"While I was in Manhattan, I asked my team how they felt about starting another BioTech office in Sapphire Bay. I've never seen so many people excited to move to another part of the country."

Katie's mouth dropped open. "You'd move here? For me?"

"Unless you're prepared to stay here or move to New York City, I can't see any way we can be together."

"The Writers in Residence Program is only for six months. I could come back after that and—"

"The last two weeks felt like a lifetime. Six months will be worse."

The door swung open and Zac carried another box into the kitchen. "It's so cold outside I'm sure I've got frostbite. Is the coffee hot?"

Peter looked down at the coffeepot. He hadn't even plugged it in. "Not yet."

Zac's gaze moved from Peter to Katie and back again. "You're discussing something important, aren't you?"

Katie sent him a strained smile. "It's okay. I was about to leave, anyway."

Peter's heart pounded. "We need to talk about what—"

"It won't change anything. I'll call you when I get back from Los Angeles."

And with her chin held high, she left the kitchen.

Zac waited until they heard the click of the front door before saying anything. "That didn't sound promising."

"It wasn't supposed to. She's moving back to Los Angeles."

"Without you?"

Peter nodded. He couldn't imagine his life without Katie but, somehow, he would have to try.

THE REST of the week flew by. Before Katie knew it, she'd been to Los Angeles, met the editorial team at Plumridge Books, and spoken to some of the staff from the art department at UCLA. It was a whirlwind visit that was everything she'd wanted her life to be before her grandma died. Now all she had to do was decide if it was what she still wanted.

"Earth to Katie. Is anyone there?"

She looked into Diana's smiling face. "Sorry. What did you say?"

"The oven timer's beeping. Do you want me to—"

Katie didn't wait for her sister to say anything else. Rushing out of the dining room, she flew into the kitchen. Daydreaming about her trip to California wouldn't save the croissants she was baking.

Charlie lifted his head off his paws as she turned off the timer and opened the oven door. Breathing a sigh of relief, she carefully slid the baking sheets onto two wooden chopping boards. A dozen golden croissants made the kitchen smell like one of the small French patisseries she'd visited on her one and only trip to Paris.

"Yum. They look delicious." Diana picked up her bowl of granola and sat beside Charlie. "You haven't told me about Los Angeles. Did you enjoy seeing your friends again?"

"I did, but it felt strange."

"In what way?"

Katie checked the time before taking a jar of peaches out of the cupboard. "When my friends told me about what they've been doing, it was almost as if we lived on different planets. Some of the things I thought were important before I left Los Angeles don't matter anymore."

"Is that a good thing?"

"In some ways. It wasn't until I was back there that I realized how much simpler my life is in Sapphire Bay."

Diana helped herself to some peaches. "Not having to work as a waitress must make a big difference?"

Katie looked around the inn's gleaming white kitchen. "I'd bake tasty breakfast dishes for our guests forever if I could. It's much more rewarding than waitressing."

"Do you remember when Grandma used to teach us how to bake? Out of all of us, you were the only one who came back after dinner for another lesson. I always thought you'd open your own café or bakery."

"I did too, but renting space anywhere is expensive." She frowned at her sister. On the same day Katie had flown to Los Angeles, Diana and Ethan had left for a short honeymoon in Vancouver. Their entire family had enjoyed dinner with them last night, but Katie hadn't expected to see her sister here so early.

"I thought you'd be enjoying your first day back in Sapphire Bay with Ethan?"

"He had to go into work early and I promised Barbara I'd take the Ackermans to St. Ignatius. They're looking forward to visiting the Three Chiefs Cultural Center."

"I thought it burned down last year?"

"It did, but it's been moved to a large log cabin." Leaning her elbows on the table, Diana watched Katie move around the kitchen. "What did Peter say when you told him you're moving back to California?"

Her hand paused in front of the cutlery drawer. "He doesn't want me to go."

"That wouldn't surprise anyone."

"He's thinking of opening an office in Sapphire Bay."

"For BioTech Industries?"

Katie nodded.

Diana's eyes widened. "He must have been serious about spending more time with you."

Thinking about how Peter felt about her had kept Katie awake for most of the night. "I don't know what to do. I never thought I'd live in Sapphire Bay permanently. Even coming back to fulfill the terms of Grandma's will wasn't easy."

"I know what you mean. After my first marriage ended, I came back here to find who I was again. I never thought I'd meet anyone I could love, but then I met Ethan and everything fell into place. It wasn't so easy for him, though. He changed his life so we could be together."

Katie thought about Peter's family, his company, and what he was prepared to do to spend more time with her. For someone who'd always valued her independence, who didn't want to rely on anyone else, the sacrifices he was willing to make were just as overwhelming as leaving the life she'd known in California.

"If I go back to Los Angeles, the writers in residence position and the contract with Plumridge Books will give me a steady income for the next twelve months."

"And after that?"

"Hopefully, the publishing house will ask me to write more books."

Diana placed her bowl and spoon in the dishwasher. "I hope they do. But, if they don't, you'll be back at square one, working in your friend's restaurant and trying to write as often as you can." She checked her watch, then leaned in and hugged Katie. "I need to meet the Ackermans in the entry-way. I'm sure whatever you decide to do will work out in the end."

It wasn't the end Katie was worried about. It was how she would get there and how long it would take. It was expensive living in Los Angeles and, if there was one thing she'd realized a long time ago, it was that money didn't grow on trees. Or in the pockets of waitresses.

PENNY TURNED her laptop around and Katie peered at the screen. "I can't believe Grandma's old wooden chest looks so good."

"It took a lot longer than Chloe thought to restore it," Barbara said from the far end of the sofa. Leaning forward, she pointed to the brass hinges. "Everything has been restored, right down to the lock and hinges."

Chloe had sent them a selection of photos that were in the catalog for the exhibition at the Smithsonian. Katie couldn't believe how amazing everything looked. Even her great-grandmother's journals showed just how much care had been taken to preserve them.

"I'm glad we let the Smithsonian have everything in the chest." Katie scrolled to the next image. "There's no way we could have looked after each piece as well as they have."

Barbara moved closer. "Is that the embroidered baby gown Grandma was wearing in the photo we found? The one in front of the steamboat in Polson?"

Penny frowned. "It looks like it. It's beautiful."

Katie sighed. "This all seems so surreal. Before Grandma died, we hardly knew anything about our great-grandparents. Now look at us."

Charlie woofed from the doorway.

Barbara smiled. "Even Charlie agrees with you."

Katie frowned. He must have rushed ahead and come inside using his doggy door.

Instead of flopping in the middle of the floor like he usually did, he barked again.

It was so unlike him that Katie got off the sofa and walked toward him. "What's wrong, boy?"

Turning toward the door, he looked over his wide shoulders to make sure she was following him.

"Something's wrong," she told her sisters.

Barbara picked up her cell phone. "I'll call Diana. She usually puts Charlie on his leash when they walk around the streets."

"I'll get our hats and jackets." Penny rushed back to the mudroom.

Charlie headed outside. Katie grabbed a spare jacket from the coat stand and the emergency kit they kept in a closet. She followed their Golden Lab and carefully walked down the garden path toward the road. Usually, by this time of the evening, Penny and Diana were at home with their husbands. But it had been so busy they'd decided to have a glass of wine together at the end of the day.

Diana had left the inn half an hour ago to take Charlie for a walk. It was cold and dark, but that was nothing new for this time of the year.

Penny and Barbara caught up to Katie just as she was stepping onto the sidewalk.

"Thank goodness she didn't walk around the lake," Barbara said as she held her cell phone to her ear. "Diana's phone went straight to voicemail and Ethan isn't answering his phone."

"Try Theo's," Katie said quickly. "Diana said he was going to the gym with Ethan after work." She kept glancing at Barbara, waiting for Theo to answer his phone.

"Nothing. I'll call the gym."

Penny grabbed hold of Barbara's arm as she slipped across the icy sidewalk. "Be careful."

"I'm trying. Why don't men answer their phones? It's not a big deal. All they have to do is take it with them and leave it on." She growled low in her throat. "No one's answering the gym phone, either."

"She can't be too far away." But the farther they walked, the more concerned Katie became.

Barbara held her cell phone up to her ear. "Hi. It's Barbara Terry. Can you find Ethan Preston for me? It's an emergency...He isn't? What about Theo Olson? He was supposed to be at the gym tonight, too."

It seemed to take forever before Barbara spoke again. "Okay. Thanks for looking." She dropped her cell phone into her pocket and sighed. "They must have decided to do something else. They never arrived at the gym."

Penny's face turned white. "Where's Charlie going?" He'd veered off the sidewalk and was heading around the corner to an old abandoned garage. "If he's following Diana, why would she have gone this way?"

Katie walked faster. "I don't know, but it's too cold to be out here for long." All kinds of horrible images were swirling through her head and none of them ended well.

Stopping in front of the garage doors, Katie yelled through a smashed wooden panel. "Diana! Are you here?"

Barbara and Penny waited beside her, listening intently for any reply.

When they heard nothing, Katie knelt beside Charlie. "Where's Diana?"

Their lovable, slightly ditsy dog licked her face, then trotted around the side of the building. Everyone followed him.

Katie prayed he hadn't forgotten what they were doing

out here. Turning on her cell phone's flashlight, she scanned the backyard. "Diana!"

"Over here."

Barbara rushed toward a high mound of snow backed up against the building. "Diana?"

"In here."

Katie had never been so glad to hear her voice. She hurried after Barbara, skidding to a stop at the entrance to what looked like a small shed. Diana was inside, sitting on the ground with her back against the wall and her legs in front of her. Tucked against her chest and wrapped in her jacket, was a child.

Penny was already on the phone, calling the emergency services.

Barbara took off her gloves and jacket and helped Diana put them on. "What happened?"

"I was walking Charlie and heard someone crying."

Katie knelt on the other side of Diana and touched the child's face. Familiar, sleepy blue eyes stared back at her. "Adele?"

A slight nod of the child's head made Katie's breath catch. "Are you hurt, honey?"

The six-year-old shook her head.

"She's cold but okay," Diana said through chattering teeth. "I fell over a pipe that was covered in snow. I've twisted my ankle."

Penny came into the shed. "The paramedics are at least half an hour away. Zac's on call at the medical clinic, so they're sending him. He should be here soon."

Katie unzipped the emergency kit and wrapped a survival blanket around Diana and Adele. "We'd better have a look at your ankle."

"It's the left one. I can't put any weight on it. Even when I try to move, it's painful."

Carefully, Barbara and Katie lifted the leg of her wet jeans.

Barbara's gaze shot to Katie.

The swelling and bruising looked a lot worse than any sprain Katie had seen. "It doesn't look too bad," she lied. "Zac will be here soon to look after you."

Barbara cleared her throat. "I'll make another call to see how far away he is."

Katie knew she would be doing a lot more than that. "Tell them Adele's last name is Quentin," she said softly. Hopefully, the police would let her parents know she was okay. Having a child disappear must be a parent's worst nightmare. For it to happen in the middle of winter would be terrifying.

As soon as Barbara left, Charlie sat beside Diana. Her hand reached out and she patted his back. "Good boy."

"Did you send him home to find us?"

Diana nodded. "My cell phone's dead. I didn't know what else to do."

Katie hugged her sister. "You did the right thing." Before she moved away, she felt Diana's skin. She was still as cold as ice but, hopefully, once she was in the medical clinic, she'd be okay. Thanks to Diana's jacket, Adele was a lot warmer. "Do you know why Adele was here?"

"She saw a mouse and followed him."

"It was Mindy," Adele whispered.

Katie touched Adele's cheek. The white mouse from her stories was always having adventures. It didn't surprise her that Adele had followed a real mouse. In her imagination, Mindy was as real as her other pets. What did shock her was how far she'd walked. "You'll have a wonderful story to tell everyone in our writing group."

A sleepy sigh was the only response she got. "Try and stay awake, honey."

Diana groaned as Adele moved on her lap. "We've been singing songs."

"Twinkle, twinkle, little star. That's my favorite."

Katie touched Diana's shoulder. "Do you want me to hold Adele?"

"It's okay," her sister whispered. "We're keeping each other warm."

Penny checked her watch. "I'll wait outside for Zac. He can't be too far away."

Katie nodded. With Diana and Adele looking increasingly pale, she didn't know what to do. By the time Barbara came back into the shed, she was shivering more than Diana.

"Here," Katie said as she took off her jacket. "Put this on. Dad's jacket is a lot warmer than the sweater you're wearing."

"But you'll get cold."

"Not as cold as you are." For the first time in a long while, Barbara didn't argue. "Wait here with Diana and Adele. I'll keep Penny company."

"She's on the sidewalk."

Katie stayed clear of the mounds of snow piled around the shed. If the pipe Diana had tripped over was here, she didn't want to risk doing the same thing.

As she trudged through the snow, her head lifted when she heard sirens. Thankfully, they were coming this way.

CHAPTER 19

*E*than rushed into the medical clinic. "Where's Diana?"

Katie pointed to the hallway behind them. "Second door on the left." Before she'd finished speaking, he was hurtling toward the room Zac had taken Diana into.

Adele's parents had arrived ten minutes ago, looking pale and anxious. Katie had sat with their daughter until they arrived. With her small body wrapped in heated blankets, a warm intravenous solution circulating through her body, and an oxygen mask helping to warm her airways, Zac was doing everything he could to help her.

Charlie was sitting in front of her and she gave him another hug. Without him, Adele and Diana could have died.

The door opened again and Mabel and Allan arrived.

"How's Diana?" her dad asked.

"She's okay, but Zac wants to transfer her to Polson with Adele. Ethan just arrived."

Mabel looked down the hallway. "Can we go in and see her?"

"Give Ethan a few minutes," Allan said softly. "We can talk to her later."

Katie could see her mom was torn between wanting to see Diana and letting Ethan look after her. "She'll be okay, Mom."

"How's her ankle?"

"Zac X-rayed it and it's broken. An orthopedic surgeon will look at it in Polson."

"Oh, my," Mabel sat beside Katie.

"Barbara and Penny are getting everyone a cup of hot chocolate. They shouldn't be too far away."

Allan sat on the other side of Katie and gave Charlie a hug. "Who's a good boy?"

Charlie started panting and his eyes closed in ecstasy as he enjoyed every moment of his hug.

When her dad sat back in the chair, Charlie settled at his feet. "Barbara told us what happened. She said Charlie led you to the old garage."

"When he arrived at the inn without Diana, we knew something was wrong. He took us straight to the shed." Katie's eyes filled with tears. "What if we'd left the inn? We'd talked about going to Penny's house, but Wyatt's in the middle of a painting and we didn't want to disturb him."

Her dad's hand squeezed hers. "There's no point worrying about what might have happened. It didn't, and that's all that matters. Charlie just might have saved Diana and the little girl's life."

Taking a deep breath, Katie clamped her lips together to stop them from trembling. She wanted to tell her dad the little girl's name was Adele but, if she said anything, she'd burst into tears.

When the door opened again, she was shocked to see Peter. He looked as white as a sheet.

"Thank goodness you're okay."

She stepped into his open arms and buried her face against his jacket.

His arms tightened around her in a fierce hug. "Theo told me what happened. Will Adele and Diana be all right?"

Katie nodded. "I think so. Diana's broken some of the bones in her ankle, so she'll need to see another doctor." Hot, salty tears stung her eyes. "She was in so much pain."

Instead of telling her everything would be okay, he held her close, waiting for the wave of emotion to pass.

"It's just as well we bought extra drinks," Penny said from the doorway in a voice that was far too cheerful. She smiled at Katie. "Sip this. It'll make you feel better."

Katie wiped her eyes and took the takeout cup. "Thanks."

Barbara handed her parents a cup of hot chocolate each, before passing one to Peter. "Theo and Wyatt will be here in a few minutes. We bought extra drinks if anyone else arrives."

Mabel left her cup on the coffee table. "Ethan's with Diana and the little girl's parents are here, too."

Penny sat on the edge of a chair. "Does anyone know how far away the ambulance is?"

Katie shook her head. "Zac will know, but I haven't seen him since we arrived."

"It can't be too far away," Barbara muttered. "I could call the emergency dispatchers and ask them?"

"It doesn't matter," Mabel said. "It'll be here as soon as it can."

A worried silence settled over the waiting room.

Allan moved seats to be closer to his wife and Peter sat beside Katie, holding her hand.

It wasn't until Ethan came down the hallway to see if Mabel and Allan wanted to see Diana, that their mom cried.

And within seconds, Katie, Penny, and Barbara were crying, too.

LEEANNA MORGAN

❄

FORTY MINUTES LATER, Peter walked into The Lakeside Inn with Katie. "Would you like a hot drink?"

"No, thanks. If I have any more caffeine or chocolate, I won't sleep." She stopped in the entryway and held his hands. "Thank you for meeting us at the clinic. It meant a lot to have you there."

"I couldn't do much, but I'm glad you're happy I was there."

Katie's eyes filled with tears. "I'll always be happy that you care."

Peter had to stop himself from wrapping her in his arms. In a few weeks, she was moving to Los Angeles and there was a high chance he wouldn't see her again. But even knowing their time together was limited, he couldn't stop wanting to be with her.

He kissed her forehead. "You're exhausted. Come with me." With his hand still holding hers, he led her through to the private living room. "Sit down and tell me what's wrong."

Taking a deep breath, she wiped her eyes and looked at the rocking chairs opposite them. "Finding Diana and Adele made me realize how fragile life is. Everything Diana has ever done, all the things she wants to do, could have been wiped out in an instant if Charlie hadn't found her. It made me think about my life and what's important."

Peter wrapped his arm around Katie's shoulders and pulled her close. While they were in the clinic, she hadn't said much, but he'd felt the turmoil building inside of her. She needed time to talk about what had happened and how she was feeling without the weight of her family's anxiety overwhelming her.

"Did I tell you that Grandma used to spend a lot of time in this room?"

198

Peter shook his head. "No, but I can see why. It's an amazing space." In the daylight, with its floor to ceiling windows placed around a semi-circular wall, the view of the lake and mountains would be spectacular.

"My grandparents would sit in front of the windows and watch the sunrise from their rocking chairs. Without fail, Granddad always told Grandma how much he loved her. After he died, the roses he'd planted were her connection to him. She would sit in her chair with a vase of roses on a table beside her, watching the world wake up. She missed him, but she said it made her happy knowing he was waiting for her. I'm grateful I was part of their lives."

"It sounds like they had a happy marriage."

Katie lifted her head off his shoulder and smiled. "They had their moments. Grandma was the sweetest person, but she had a fiery temper. Granddad liked telling her what to do, which didn't go down too well. But, despite their differences, they loved each other. I want the same kind of connection with the person I love, the ability to be myself regardless of what that is."

He pushed a stray lock of hair over her ear and smiled when the curl bounced back to where it used to be. "I want that, too. I think most people do. Do you want to know something? You're one of the few women I've met who don't want anything from me. Other than when you asked Zac to make sure I wore an elf costume to the Santa parade."

A blush heated her pale cheeks. "How did you find out?"

"Willow told me."

A sparkle returned to Katie's eyes. "You have to admit you looked cute *and* you enjoyed handing out the candy."

"I'm not sure about the cute part, but I liked giving people the candy. That's not all I enjoyed. After the parade, we went back to the church for a drink and a slice of Shelley's apple pie. That's when I realized how special you are and how much I care about you."

Katie's eyes filled with tears. "We hadn't known each other for very long, but I felt the same way. What are we going to do?"

"I don't know, but we'll think of something."

Katie yawned. "I'm sorry. My brain feels like mush. Everything must be catching up with me."

Peter kissed her cheek. "It's time I went home, anyway. Are you sure you'll be okay?"

"I'll be fine. Penny's next door and Barbara's staying at the inn tonight."

He was still worried about leaving her here, even with her sister keeping her company. "Do you have many guests?"

"Ten, but they're no bother. All I have to do is prepare breakfast for them tomorrow and do some housework." She sent him a tired smile. "I'll be okay. After a good night's sleep, everyone will feel better."

As they were walking toward the front door, Katie sighed. "I don't want to lose what we have, Peter."

"Neither do I. Whatever happens, I want you to know I love you."

"I love you, too."

After wrapping her in a hug, he opened the front door and walked outside. Katie wasn't the only person who felt like tonight had changed her life forever. When Theo called to tell him what had happened, he'd panicked and imagined the worst. It wasn't until he saw Katie and heard that everyone was okay, that he'd calmed down.

Before the accident, he never would have moved to Los Angeles. Now, every reason why that couldn't happen seemed unimportant. What *was* important was Katie. He'd do anything he could to make her happy, even if it meant moving his entire company to California. He loved her more than anyone or anything in the world, and that was something he wouldn't take for granted.

As he turned toward his truck, he sniffed the cold night air. The sweet scent of roses filled his lungs.

With a smile, he looked back at the inn. Maybe, in the mysterious way the universe worked, that was Katie's grandma's way of telling him she approved.

"I DON'T THINK you should be doing that." Katie grabbed the sack of flour out of Diana's hands. "The doctor said you have to rest."

Diana scowled. "I'll go crazy if I sit around the house doing nothing." She pointed to the kitchen stool and the mixing bowl and spoons sitting on the counter. "After I've found the ingredients, everything's ready to go. Before you know it, I'll have fresh cookies waiting for our guests when they come home."

"Ethan dropped you off on the condition you didn't do too much."

"I'm not."

Katie didn't miss the stubborn tilt to Diana's jaw. Three days wasn't nearly long enough to be bored, but stranger things had happened in the last few weeks. Thankfully, Diana's broken bones hadn't required surgery, but she did need to wear a walking boot and use crutches. "I don't think Ethan imagined you baking for our guests when he left you here."

All the fire left Diana's eyes. "You have to give me something to do. Even Charlie's sick of watching TV with me."

"I know it isn't easy but, if you don't do what your doctor said, your ankle won't heal properly." Katie looked around the kitchen. There had to be some way of making it easier for her sister. "If you sit at the kitchen table, I'll bring the ingredients to you. You'll be able to do everything from there, except place the cookie dough in the oven."

The relieved smile on Diana's face was good to see. "Thank you. I knew you'd help me."

"Don't thank me too soon. The kitchen table works equally well as an ironing board. You can iron the linens after you've finished the cookies."

"That sounds perfect."

Barbara stuck her head around the edge of the doorframe. "Chloe called me on Zoom. Do you want to speak to her about the exhibition?"

"Can you bring your laptop in here?" Diana asked.

"Good idea. I'll be back in a couple of minutes."

While Diana made herself comfortable at the table, Katie picked up the recipe her sister was using. "Chocolate, macadamia, and cranberry cookies? Are you sure you want to start with something this fancy?"

"It's one of Megan's recipes from Sweet Treats. I could do something else if you don't have some of the ingredients."

"I'd have to buy macadamia nuts, but that wouldn't be a problem if you really want to bake them." Taking a folder out of a drawer, she handed it to Diana. "After we've spoken to Chloe, look through here. These are the cookies I've already made for our guests."

"I'm back." Barbara placed the laptop in the middle of the table and turned it around for Diana.

After Katie sat beside her sisters, she waved at Chloe's smiling face. "It's good to see you. It seems like it's been months since we last talked."

"You can say that again. Barbara told me you've been offered a publishing contract. Congratulations."

"Thanks. I'm still deciding what I'll do, but it was interesting visiting the publishing house." Katie didn't dare look at her sisters. She could already feel the weight of Barbara's stare pinning her to the chair.

"And what about you, Diana? Barbara said you found a missing child."

"We sort of bumped into each other. Luckily, Charlie knew where to find me when I couldn't get home."

"How's the ankle?"

"Sore but bearable. What about you?"

Chloe sighed. "I'm busy organizing two more exhibitions and coordinating the restoration of another three projects. Sometimes, I feel like a mouse on one of those wheels that spin around and around but never go anywhere."

Barbara frowned. "It sounds like you need a vacation. You should visit us in Sapphire Bay and stay at the inn as our guest."

"That sounds like bliss, but I'll be okay. I think I've got a case of winteritis. As soon as the sun shines, I'll be back to my usual bossy self. Did you look at the photos I sent you?"

Katie nodded. "We did. They're amazing."

"That's because what we're displaying is gorgeous. We were so lucky that each piece was in such good condition. I emailed Barbara the invitations for your family. Do you have them?"

Barbara nodded. "I've printed them and placed them inside our travel folder."

Diana's eyes widened. "We have a travel folder?"

"We have a folder for everything," Katie said with a grin.

"I'm not that bad," Barbara growled. "Especially compared to Penny."

Chloe laughed. "You're a woman after my own heart. Dad gave me a color-coded set of plastic folders with Post-Its and fluorescent highlighters for Christmas. I couldn't have been happier."

Katie opened a document on her cell phone and looked

up at Chloe. "If anyone gave me a set of folders, I wouldn't know what to do with them."

Diana grinned. "You could donate them to Penny or Barbara."

Barbara cleared her throat. "A woman can never have enough folders. Katie, did you have some questions you wanted to ask Chloe?"

"I do." After tapping on her cell phone, she opened a list of the questions she'd thought of. "Is it okay to ask them now or do you want me to email them to you?"

"If there are only a few, ask me now."

Barbara leaned sideways and looked at Katie's phone. "Who's more organized now?"

"Some of them are Mom's questions."

"Of course, they are," Barbara said.

"It's true. Here's her first one. Can we take photos at the opening of the exhibition and post them on Facebook?"

Chloe nodded. "That's more than okay. The only thing you won't be able to do is take photos if you want to see the exhibition before opening night."

Diana sat taller in the chair. "We can do that?"

"It's all ready, so I don't see why not. Either myself or someone in my team would have to go with you, but it can be arranged. I could even give you a behind-the-scenes tour of how we restore the furniture and other things that come into my department. When do you arrive in Washington, D.C.?"

"At 4pm on February 10."

Chloe looked as though she was opening something on her computer. "I can spend a few hours with you on the afternoon of the 11th if you'd like to meet me at the Smithsonian?"

Katie looked at Barbara and Diana. They both seemed excited by the idea. "Book us in for whatever time suits you.

I'll check with the rest of our family to see if they want to come."

With a nod, Chloe tapped something on her keyboard. "I've booked you in and you should have a meeting request waiting for you in your inboxes. All I'll need is the final number of people who are coming before we meet. What's next?"

After another ten minutes, Katie had the answers to the questions she needed. With their accommodation booked, sightseeing options identified, and a behind-the-scenes tour of the National Museum of American History organized, she couldn't have been happier.

"If you have any other questions, let me know."

"We will," Barbara said before they ended the call. "We'll see you soon."

"I'm looking forward to it."

And with a push of a button, Barbara ended the call. "That was exciting."

Diana closed the lid of the laptop and handed it to Barbara. "I hope my ankle's okay by then."

Katie picked up her cell phone. She was beginning to think she was just as bad as her sisters at organizing things. "I saw Zac yesterday and asked him about traveling with a broken ankle. He suggested a few things that might make the trip to Washington, D.C. easier." She showed her sisters the pictures of the mobility scooters and knee walkers. "Either of these would work. The rental companies will deliver them to our hotel. You wouldn't need to use them all the time, but they might help. Especially if you want to do a lot of sightseeing."

Diana studied the photos. "I like the idea of the mobility scooter. There's even an area where I could put my shopping."

"I'll send you the link to the website and leave it with you to organize." Katie slid her cell phone into her pocket. "Are you ready to bake some cookies?"

Barbara cleared her throat. "There's something else we need to discuss. What did you mean when you said you're deciding what you'll do about the publishing contract? Are you considering not doing the three-book deal?"

Katie frowned. "I still have a few days before I need to let Plumridge Books know what I'm doing. In the meantime, I'm keeping my options open."

Diana sent her a beaming smile. "Good for you."

Barbara studied Katie's face. "Good luck. It won't be an easy decision to make."

Katie sighed. If anything, it was the easiest one she'd ever had to make.

CHAPTER 20

*P*eter walked into one of the meeting rooms at The Welcome Center. Normally, the entire complex was a hive of activity, with people moving between the accommodation wings and the communal living spaces. But, for some reason, the facility was almost deserted.

Katie had asked him to meet her here and it wasn't like her to be late. Given the time, he'd assumed she would be finishing her writing group meeting, but it looked as though he was wrong. Maybe they'd finished early to enjoy cookies and hot chocolate in the dining area? He checked the time, then headed into the corridor.

He looked in the kitchen and the dining room, then through the windows and into the backyard. No one was there.

Checking his phone, he scrolled through his emails and texts, looking for any message she might have sent him. With nothing there either, he returned to the main reception desk. Andrea was busy on the phone, so he waited on the other side of the desk.

"Hi, Peter," she said as she slid the phone onto its charger.

"The phone has been ringing nonstop since I started work. How can I help you?"

He heard someone running toward him and he turned to see Katie's bright red hair bobbing in time with her steps. "It's okay. Katie's found me."

"Sorry I'm late." She wrapped her arms around his waist and kissed him soundly on the lips. "You smell nice."

He grinned at her dreamy smile. "I'll have to wear my new aftershave more often if you like it so much."

Andrea cleared her throat. "Enough of that lovey-dovey talk. But, from another single woman's perspective, your aftershave is very appealing."

A blush worked its way up Peter's neck. It didn't help that Katie was grinning at him as if he was a tasty morsel she'd like to nibble.

The phone rang again. "Gotta go," Andrea said as she reached for the phone. "Enjoy the presentations."

Peter looked at Katie. "Presentations? I thought you had a writing group meeting."

"There was a change of plans." Holding his hand, she pulled him in the direction she'd come from. "You won't want to miss what's happening. Come on."

Whatever presentations were underway, Katie was keen to get there quickly. "What are we going to see?"

"It's something special." Katie stopped outside a set of double doors. "I know you're not much of a publicity kind of guy, and you definitely don't like to be in the spotlight. So, whatever happens behind these doors will be done in the strictest of confidence. Pastor John has already started, so we'll sneak into the back of the room. Don't worry. There are plenty of chairs."

The number of chairs was the least of Peter's worries. He had a feeling Katie was about to show him something he wouldn't like.

Pushing open one of the doors, she tightened the grip on his hand and pulled him inside. At least ten rows of chairs faced a raised platform. John stood in the middle of the stage, talking to a crowd of adults and teenagers.

"We can sit here," Katie whispered as they sat in the back row. "Can you see everything?"

He nodded and sent her a confused look. "Why are we here?"

"You'll see."

Peter had never liked surprises. He looked around the audience, hoping something would give him a better idea of what was happening.

As his gaze scanned the audience, he stopped at a teenager wearing a bright red shirt with the image of a Christmas tree showing on the back. He looked familiar, but it was hard to figure out where he'd seen him. Two rows behind the first boy, another was wearing the same shirt. They must have come here straight from work to…Suddenly, he realized why they were here. He turned to Katie.

She held her finger to her lips. "Wait until the end."

John had promised he wouldn't tell anyone about the donations his company had made to the church. In Peter's mind, that included the scholarships.

Everyone in the audience clapped as five teenagers made their way to the front of the room. They look as confused as Peter was when Katie had brought him here.

As the last teenager stood on the stage, John spoke to the audience. "With another year underway, I wanted to thank you for the kindness and generosity you've shown to everyone in our community. The last twelve months have brought challenges no one expected. But knowing we're part of a community who cares about each other is changing people's lives. For some, it's the difference between having a good day and not being able to get out of bed. For others, it gives them the courage to face some of the issues that brought them here."

Peter thought about the men and women he'd met in the tiny home village. People like Richard, who'd been in situations that left him physically and emotionally broken. Slowly, they were rebuilding their lives. They were creating brighter futures for themselves and their families. Futures that wouldn't be possible without a safe place to call home.

"As part of our commitment to caring about each other," John continued, "we've been given the opportunity to support five outstanding young people in their journey through life. In their own unique ways, they've made us proud of who they are." He turned to the teenagers. "Nate, Marcus, Sally, Jessie, and Juliette. You've helped a lot of people feel good about living here. We know the next stage of each of your lives will have challenges, and we want to help. Enclosed in each of these envelopes is a registration form that will give you full scholarships to Montana State University. From our hearts to yours, we hope this helps you to continue to make a difference in the world."

Peter's eyes filled with tears as each of the teenager's stunned expressions turned from disbelief to joy. Whether they knew it or not, the scholarships would be a stepping stone to so many opportunities.

A warm hand wrapped around his. "You did good, Mr. Bennett," Katie whispered.

"No one was supposed to know it was me."

Katie's smile disappeared. She looked around the room. If she was waiting for the clapping and cheering to stop before she said anything, they could be here for a while. As if thinking the same thing, she held his hand and nodded toward the doors.

As soon as they were in the hallway, she took a deep

breath. "Don't be upset. I only found out by accident. I was speaking to Shelley when someone from MSU called her."

"Does anyone else know?"

She shook her head. "When I told Shelley what I suspected, she made me promise not to say anything to anyone else."

A sick feeling settled in Peter's stomach. "When did you find out?"

"Before the Santa Parade."

That was more than a month ago.

"I didn't say anything because you didn't want anyone to know about the scholarships. If I'd told you, you might have withdrawn your offer."

"I wouldn't have done that."

"I know that now, but I didn't know it then."

Her logical argument for not saying anything made sense, but he was still disappointed. "Did Shelley tell you about the other donation BioTech made?"

Katie's eyes widened. "There's more?"

He watched her closely. "BioTech's sponsoring all the programs the church runs for the next twelve months. It'll free up John's time to help people instead of fundraising."

"That's amazing. But are you sure? I mean, I know Pastor John will be thrilled, but you must be donating a lot of money."

The meeting room doors opened and Peter looked over Katie's shoulder. Thankfully, it was a mother and her young daughter and not the room full of people they'd just left.

Katie waited until the woman had walked away. "When John asked if I thought you'd want to be here today, I said yes. Was I right?"

Reluctantly, Peter nodded.

"Don't worry," Katie said seriously. "I won't treat you any differently because you have a good heart."

"What if I'm worried you only like me because I have a lot of money?"

Her eyes widened. "I've already told you money isn't important to me."

"Then why are you going back to Los Angeles?"

Katie sighed. "I'm not."

"What?"

"I'm not going back. I've told my agent I'm accepting the three-book contract, but I'm not doing the Writers in Residence Program. If other authors can write from anywhere in the world, I can do it from Sapphire Bay."

Peter's heart pounded. "You were so sure you wanted to live in California. What changed?"

"You." Katie held his hands. "Instead of being hundreds of miles apart, I want to spend the next six months with you. If I was in Los Angeles, we'd be living separate lives. That isn't good for any relationship."

Pulling her close, he wrapped her in his arms and held her tight. Even though it was everything he wanted, he was still worried she'd regret her decision. "Are you one hundred percent sure that's what you want to do?"

Katie kissed him and grinned. "I'm three hundred percent sure. And if you invite me over for mugs of hot chocolate on your front porch, I'll be even happier."

Peter's entire world was focused on the incredible woman standing in his arms. "You can come to my house any time you want. I love you, Katie."

With a happy sigh that came straight from her heart, she snuggled closer. "I love you, too."

THREE WEEKS LATER, Katie unlocked the back door of the inn and waited for her noisy family to arrive. Last year, as soon as Chloe had given them a date for their great-grandparents exhibition, they'd made sure they wouldn't have any bookings while they were away.

Unfortunately, it didn't make their lives any easier. After their last guests had left, Katie and her sisters had been busy making sure everything was in tip-top shape for their next arrivals on Tuesday morning.

After falling into bed at midnight, she wasn't looking forward to leaving at six o'clock the following morning. But, here she was, pouring granola into a bowl and hoping the rest of her family had set their alarm clocks.

A quick tap on the door signaled the beginning of the rush. "Are you awake, Katie?" Penny yelled from the mudroom.

"I'm in the kitchen."

A smiling face appeared around the edge of the doorframe. "I thought you might have slept in."

"I'm too excited for that. Where's Wyatt?"

"I'm here," came a muffled reply. A few seconds later, he appeared with two suitcases in his hands. "Where do you want our luggage?"

"Leave them by the front door. We can stack them in the vehicles once everyone's here."

Penny placed a clipboard on the kitchen counter. "I worked out how many suitcases we can fit into each of the vehicles we're taking to the airport. As long as everyone sticks to the numbers they gave me, we should be fine."

If it were up to Katie, she'd just squeeze them in, but Penny had a plan for every occasion. "Sounds good. Have you called Diana and Ethan?"

"They were awake and having breakfast half an hour ago. Mom called me, so she's awake. Theo called Wyatt to check a few facts for a story he's writing, so he's awake. That only leaves Peter."

"I'm here, too."

Katie left her bowl of granola on the counter and walked into the mudroom. "Good morning. Did you get much sleep last night?"

"I finished work at one o'clock this morning." He kissed her soundly on the lips and smiled. "But that's okay. It means I'll be ready for my meetings in Manhattan."

Instead of flying with them, Peter was taking a slightly later flight to New York City. On Friday afternoon, he'd travel to Washington, D.C., speak to some potential investors, then meet them at the Smithsonian for the opening of their great-grandparent's exhibition.

Katie held his hand. "Have you had breakfast? I made a batch of your favorite muffins before I went to bed."

"I had some toast, but I won't say no to a muffin."

Penny walked into the mudroom and hung up her jacket. "You'd better be quick. Wyatt's already poured himself a cup of coffee. The muffins are next."

Without needing any extra prompting, Peter hurried into the kitchen.

In the space of ten minutes, The Lakeside Inn went from serene, early morning tranquility, to chaos.

Katie watched Penny's worst nightmare unfold. Their mom had packed everything except the kitchen sink. The four suitcases she'd brought with her not only upset the carefully allocated number of bags per vehicle, it would earn her parents' extra luggage fees.

Barbara's arrival did nothing to calm an already excited family gathering. Although she encouraged their mom to downsize, nothing she said or did made any difference.

After Diana hobbled into the inn, Ethan, Wyatt, Theo, and Peter began their next challenge; getting nine people, twelve suitcases, nine sets of carry-ons, and their jackets, scarves, and anything else they'd forgotten into two trucks.

By the time they were ready to leave, Katie should have been exhausted. But the thrill of seeing the exhibition, of spending five days with the people she loved, was too much.

With a grateful smile, she locked the back door and hurried down the steps.

Washington, D.C. Here we come!

CHAPTER 21

*K*atie checked her watch, then looked over the second-floor glass balustrade at the Smithsonian National Museum of American History. Peter was supposed to meet them here half an hour ago, but he still hadn't arrived.

Apart from him not being here, the rest of their visit to Washington, D.C. was going well.

Yesterday, Chloe met them at the entrance on Constitution Avenue and took them on a wonderful tour of her department.

Although most of the designers, fabricators, and model makers were based in Maryland, there was still a lot of conservation work taking place at the museum. With Katie's entire family, including her aunt, uncle, and cousins enjoying the tour, Chloe had almost needed a megaphone to be heard over the excited chatter.

"Has Peter texted you, yet?" Penny asked.

Katie shook her head. "He should be here soon. The meeting he'd organized finished an hour ago."

"The traffic in Washington, D.C. can be horrendous,"

Diana said from the wheelchair she'd borrowed. "He might be sitting in a taxi somewhere."

"He would have called if he was."

Ethan stood behind the wheelchair. "He won't be far away. We should go into the exhibition before Chloe gives her speech."

As Katie followed Diana and Ethan, she sent Peter a quick text telling him she'd meet him inside the exhibition room. She just hoped the museum hadn't locked the doors.

FLINGING OFF HIS SEATBELT, Peter sprinted toward the row of doors opening into the museum. With the rest of the building closed for general admission, he was profoundly grateful Chloe had emailed his entry pass to him. After cramming a week's worth of work into the last couple of days, he never would have remembered to bring it with him.

Before he stepped inside, a guard studied his electronic ticket and asked him for additional ID. For a moment, Peter didn't think he was going to get in. Thankfully, after a lot of consideration, the guard let him through.

Standing in the middle of the lobby was like being in a big shopping mall. To his left and right, wide corridors branched off to different exhibitions. But that wasn't where he needed to be tonight. Wasting no time, he climbed the stairs to the second floor.

It didn't matter how many times he came here, he never grew tired of seeing the silver, stylized rendition of the starspangled banner hanging on the far wall. It was huge, bold, and held his attention from whatever floor he was on.

Unfortunately, he didn't have time to admire it tonight. Checking his watch, he turned toward Unity Square and the home of the American Democracy Exhibit. The space where

Katie's great-grandparents' exhibition was being held was relatively easy to find. Especially with the large banners and red carpet directing the attendees to the correct location.

He stopped when he saw the name of the exhibit. *Lost and Found: the journey of a speech that changed the world.* Whoever had chosen the name had put a lot of thought into it. The words were poignant, laced with different meanings for Katie's family and the people who would visit the museum.

He jumped when another security guard stopped in front of him. After checking Peter's pass, he waved him forward, straight into the exhibition room.

This was the first time he'd been to an opening night. Invited guests, dressed in tuxedos and evening gowns, listened attentively as Chloe explained how a letter addressed to Robert Todd Lincoln had made its way across America to a small town in Montana. And how the words inside the letter would come to mean so much to the world.

His gaze swept across the guests, searching for Katie and her family. Mabel and her sister, Beatrice, were standing beside Allan. He scanned the faces of people he'd met at Diana's wedding; cousins and close friends who were as emotionally involved in the life of Katie's great-grandparents as she was.

As soon as he saw Katie's red hair, he smiled. She was standing on the far side of the room, between Wyatt and Penny. Her blue dress shimmered under a set of spotlights angled toward some exhibition pieces. It reminded him of the gown she'd worn to Diana's wedding.

He looked at the other side of the room and breathed a sigh of relief. The staff had remembered to place a barrier in front of the dresser where Katie's family had found the letter.

Taking a deep breath, he looked for something to take his mind off what he'd soon be doing. High on the wall behind Chloe, he found his salvation.

A copy of the Gettysburg Address, magnified for impact, hung as a reminder of why they were here. As he read the text, he paused and thought about what the words meant.

Above everything else, the speech was written to give battle-weary soldiers hope. Abraham Lincoln wanted them to know the lives of those who'd died weren't lost in vain. That it was up to everyone to continue to work toward the unification of the country and uphold democracy for all people.

Peter wondered if Abraham Lincoln realized how hard it would be to bring together a nation that had splintered in two and was struggling to move forward.

The sound of clapping yanked him out of his thoughts. Katie's ability to daydream in the middle of a crowded room must be rubbing off on him.

As everyone moved toward the start of the exhibition, he made his way through the crowd to Katie.

"You made it." Her gentle smile undid some of the knots in his stomach.

"Sorry I'm late. It took me longer to get here than I thought."

She linked her hand under his elbow. "You're here now and that's all that matters. You look handsome in your tuxedo."

Feeling even more self-conscious than usual, he touched the bow tie at his throat. "After spending so much time in Montana, I'm not used to wearing a suit. It's not as comfortable as jeans."

Ethan smiled from beside him. "Tell me about it. Diana said we'd have the shortest marriage in history if I didn't wear a suit tonight."

"Was that from the same woman who wanted you to wear a red Santa jacket to your wedding?"

"I said the same thing, but it didn't make any difference."

Katie stood on tiptoes as Chloe said something from a few feet away. "Mom and Aunt Beatrice are about to cut the ribbon. Is Dad taking some photos?"

Reaching into her pocket, Barbara pulled out her cell phone. "I don't know, but I'll take some anyway." In a flurry of red satin, she disappeared into the crowd.

After the ribbon was cut, Katie was practically jumping on the spot. "I can't wait to see everything. Is everyone ready?"

Diana looked up at Ethan. "You push through the crowd and I'll follow."

With a good-natured grin, Ethan sighed. "That just about sums up the story of my marriage."

"And it's only just begun," Diana replied.

Peter let Ethan and Diana go first. "Did Chloe show you any of the exhibition yesterday?" he asked Katie.

"No. We wanted it to be a surprise, so we only met the restoration and research teams. Did you get everything done at work?"

"Most of it. It's amazing how much I can do from Sapphire Bay. No one seemed to miss me."

Katie frowned. "Is that good or bad?"

"It should be good," Peter smiled ruefully. "But I was a little disappointed. I thought the company couldn't run without me."

"We all have that problem."

Walking into the exhibition was like stepping back in time. Chloe's team had started at the beginning of the letter's journey. They'd recreated a scene from the gambling house in Chicago when Patrick Kelly had won the letter. Tracing his footsteps, they'd traveled across America, investigating sightings of him after he'd supposedly died, and pinpointing where he'd reappeared.

Katie's eyes widened when she saw a 3D holographic

image of her great-grandfather standing in front of a steamboat with his wife. "I never realized how similar Penny is to our great-grandmother. They could have been sisters."

Peter looked at the image and then at Katie. "You have the same-shaped eyes and mouth, too."

Tilting her head to the side, Katie tried to see what he did. "Mom said the same thing. Maybe it's easier to see the resemblance in someone else."

As she moved to the next display, Peter glanced at the dresser where Katie's family had found the letter. He hoped like crazy this went well. He'd only known Katie for a few months, but he knew she was the woman he wanted to spend the rest of his life with.

And, before the end of the night, he'd know if she felt the same way, too.

KATIE LOOKED around the crowded exhibition and frowned. She wasn't superstitious and she didn't have premonitions, but she did believe in God, angels, and a beautiful place called heaven. She'd even felt the healing power of prayer. But, in all her life, she'd never been quite so aware of her grandma.

It was almost as if she was beside her, showing her the journey that had brought her into the world and made her the person she was. Even the scent of roses seemed to follow Katie, enticing her to stay a few minutes longer at different displays.

"Are you all right?"

She looked at Peter and forced a smile. "The excitement of the day must be getting to me. I keep thinking Grandma's going to suddenly appear and give everyone a guided tour of the things we found."

"From what you've said, she would have enjoyed that."

A strong scent of roses tickled Katie's nose. "Can you smell that?"

Peter sniffed. "What am I supposed to be smelling?"

"Roses. Sweet, pungent roses that almost make your eyes water."

He sniffed again and shook his head. "All I can smell is someone's perfume and it's more fruity than sweet."

Katie rubbed her nose. "It must be allergies. Have you seen Mom and Dad?"

Peter looked around the room, then froze. "They're standing in front of the dresser where you found the letter. Your dad…"

If she wasn't holding Peter's hand, she wouldn't have felt him flinch. "What's Dad doing?"

"He's bending down."

Before Katie knew what was happening, Peter pulled her across the room. Her breath caught as adrenaline surged through her body. Peter was the most level-headed person she knew. The only reason he'd move so fast was if her dad was having a heart attack or some kind of medical emergency.

"Can you still see him?" she asked as they dodged someone carrying a tray of wine glasses.

"He's—"

Her dad turned and frowned. "Has something happened? Mabel said you were rushing across the room and I thought Diana—"

"She's fine." Peter's gaze shot to the dresser. "Did you open the drawer where you found the letter?"

Allan shook his head. "Someone bumped into the rope and it fell off the stand. Mabel's going to ask Chloe why it's there. We thought her staff might still be working on the restoration."

Peter shook his head. "There's another reason it's there."

Diana, Ethan, Penny, and Wyatt joined them.

"Is everything okay?" Diana asked. "Ethan saw Peter run across the room and we thought something must have happened."

Katie was as confused as the rest of her family. "Everyone's okay. What did you think was happening, Peter?"

He took a deep breath and held her hand. "You're the reason the rope's stopping people from getting too close to the dresser."

"I am?"

"I wanted tonight to be special, not only for what your family found, but to celebrate your grandma's life. If it weren't for her, you wouldn't have come back to Sapphire Bay, and I wouldn't have met you."

By now, the crowd of people watching them had grown. Katie had no idea what Peter was doing, but Chloe was smiling as she made her way toward them, so it couldn't be too bad.

He unclipped the rope and took a pair of gloves out of his pocket. Instead of pulling them on, he turned to her and held her hands. "You weave words into stories, create worlds that children can dream about. I don't want the story of your family to end with the discovery of the letter. I'd like it to continue into forever with you beside me. I love you, Katie. When I first met you, I thought you were special. That feeling grew when I saw how kind and generous you are to the people around you. And, by the time we had Christmas together, I knew I'd love you for the rest of my life."

Katie blinked. This couldn't be happening. Peter was telling her he loved her in front of their family and friends, and total strangers who were busy taking photos of them. "I love you, too," she whispered.

Peter's hand shook as he handed her the gloves. "I bought

you a gift. Have a look in the compartment where you found the letter."

Katie bit her bottom lip. Even though her mom was dabbing tears from her eyes, she wouldn't assume Peter's gift was a ring. It was probably a pair of earrings or a bracelet. Even a necklace would fit inside the small enclosure.

Diana nudged her leg. "Take the gloves."

Nervously, she pulled on the gloves. "I'm not great around expensive furniture. I could scratch the surface or break the lovely scrollwork."

"That's why I'm here," Chloe said from beside her. "You pull the drawer open and I'll pop up the compartment."

With both sets of gloves working carefully together, Katie opened the drawer and took an envelope out of the secret compartment.

A murmur shot through the people watching them when they saw just how clever the concealed drawer was.

She frowned when she looked at Peter.

"Open it."

His softly spoken words made her heart pound. Inside the envelope was a letter and a folded handkerchief with something lumpy wrapped inside. With its embroidered corner and lace edge, it must be old.

"It was your grandma's handkerchief," Peter told her. "Your Aunt Beatrice wanted you to have it. The letter's for you to read later."

She looked at her dress and realized she didn't have any pockets. "Can you keep it safe for me?"

Peter nodded and slipped it into his jacket.

With trembling fingers, she carefully unwrapped the fine linen handkerchief. Nestled between its folds was a beautiful diamond ring.

"Oh, Peter. It's lovely."

Holding her hand, he lowered himself to one knee. With

tears in his eyes, he said, "Katie Terry. With every breath I take, I love you. Will you marry me?"

Looking into his eyes, she knew she'd finally found her soft place to fall. Peter would love her unconditionally, support her in whatever she did, and make her cups of hot chocolate when life became too much. "I will. I do. I'll marry you!"

Peter stood and pulled her into his arms. "I can't wait to marry you."

"As long as it isn't too soon," she laughed. "My family won't survive the stress of another wedding so close to Diana's and Penny's"

"Don't be so sure about that," Diana said from beside her. "I have it on good authority that Mom would be open to an Easter wedding."

"She would?"

Mabel wrapped her arms around Katie and Peter. "Don't listen to your sister. You can get married whenever you like."

"As long as we don't have to dress as rabbits," Penny added.

Katie looked up into Peter's smiling face. "My family are slightly crazy. I hope you know what you're getting yourself into."

"I'm looking forward to finding out."

And as her family and the people around them burst into applause, Katie smelled the sweet scent of her grandma's roses.

EPILOGUE

*K*atie sat quietly in her hotel room after everyone had gone to bed. The city lights of Washington, D.C. sparkled like a sea of stars, reflecting the excitement and wonder she felt inside.

She still couldn't believe Peter had asked her to marry him and share the rest of their lives together. It had been an emotional day, and it hadn't ended yet.

Before Peter went to his room, he gave her the letter he'd kept in his pocket. With a deep breath, she carefully unfolded it and began to read:

My Dearest Katie,

From the moment I met you, I knew you were someone special. Your warmth, your kindness, and your unwavering optimism have brought so much light into my life. Each day with you has been an incredible adventure, and I am endlessly grateful for every moment we have shared.

Your love for storytelling and your dedication to making the world a better place through your words inspire me more than you could ever know. Watching you bring joy and wonder into the lives of children through your books has been a true privilege.

Today, we'll be surrounded by the history and beauty of the Smithsonian. It's a reminder of how our own history has woven together so perfectly. Your grandma's legacy brought you back to Sapphire Bay, and in turn, brought us together. I can't imagine my life without you in it.

Katie, I want to spend the rest of my days making you as happy as you've made me. I want to be there for you through every high and every low, supporting you, loving you, and cherishing every moment we share.

I hope when you read this letter, you've agreed to be my wife. I know that together, we can create a beautiful life full of love, laughter, and endless adventures. You are my heart, my inspiration, and my greatest love.

With all my love,

Peter

As she finished reading, tears filled Katie's eyes, spilling over onto her cheeks. She clutched the letter to her chest, feeling a warmth spread through her heart. Peter's words echoed in her mind, and she knew without a doubt that this was the beginning of a new and beautiful chapter in their lives. She gazed out at the city lights, her heart full of love and gratitude, knowing that their future together would be as bright and breathtaking as the view before her.

THE END

THANK YOU

Thank you for reading *Christmas at Lakeside* I hope you enjoyed it! If you did...

1. Help other people find this book by **writing a review.**
2. Sign up for my **new releases e-mail**, so you can find out about the next book as soon as it's available.
3. Come like my **Facebook** page.
4. Visit my website: **leeannamorgan.com**

To discover what happens next in Sapphire Bay, keep reading to enjoy *The Flower Cottage*, Paris and Richard's story in the first book in the *The Cottages on Anchor Lane* series!

Click HERE to buy from Leeanna's Store and SAVE!

Or click HERE to purchase from other retailers.

USA TODAY BESTSELLING AUTHOR

LEEANNA
MORGAN

THE
Flower
COTTAGE

The Flower Cottage
The Cottages on Anchor Lane, Book 1

Click HERE to buy from Leeanna's Store and SAVE!

Or click HERE to purchase from other retailers.

**Fans of Robyn Carr's Virgin River series will love this
small town, feel-good romance!**

Paris Haynes has spent most of her life running from one
bad relationship to the next. Three years ago, determined to

put her past behind her, she moved to Sapphire Bay and began to rebuild her life.

Working with Kylie in the flower shop has given her a sense of purpose, a reason to live the kind of life she's always dreamed about. When she hears about the cottages that are being remodeled on Anchor Lane, she can hardly contain her excitement. She proposes a plan so outrageous, so out of her comfort zone, that she's sure it will fail before it begins.

Richard Dawkins lost his leg in Afghanistan and nearly lost his son. Moving to Sapphire Bay has given him more than a place to call home. He has new friends, a steady job, and a state-of-the-art prosthetic leg that's transformed his life.

Helping to turn the cottages on Anchor Lane into small, thriving businesses is his way of giving back to the community. But when he discovers Paris has been given the keys to the first cottage, he knows he's in trouble. With her over-the-top positivity, she's everything he doesn't need, and the only person who could change his life forever.

THE FLOWER COTTAGE is the first book in 'The Cottages on Anchor Lane' series and can easily be read as a stand-alone. All of Leeanna's series are linked. If you find a character you like, they could be in another novel. Happy reading!

Keep reading to enjoy an excerpt from ***The Flower Cottage***
the first book in *The Cottages on Anchor Lane* series!

CHAPTER 1

*P*aris placed a bouquet of pale pink roses into the refrigerator at Blooming Lovely, the only flower shop in Sapphire Bay. Three years after she'd started working with Kylie and Jackie, she still had to pinch herself to remember this wasn't a dream.

Before she'd arrived in Montana, her life was a complete mess. Now, with a little help from her friends, she finally felt as though she belonged in this small, amazing town.

"I've closed the store and put the cash into the safe. Is there anything else we need to do?" Jackie asked.

Paris opened the spreadsheet showing tomorrow's orders. "Other than printing off a list of the flowers I need from the market, we're finished for the day. Did Mrs. Smith tell you when she wants to collect her daughter's bouquet?"

"She'll be here as soon as we open."

"That's good. Have you heard from Kylie?"

"Not yet, but she should be here soon. I'll make us a hot drink while we wait."

Their boss, Kylie, was halfway through her first pregnancy and everyone was excited. This afternoon, she'd had an appointment at the medical clinic for a routine scan.

Paris checked her watch. Tomorrow morning, she was driving to Polson to re-stock their flowers. It was her favorite thing to do, even if she had to leave before sunrise to secure the best blooms.

"Sorry I'm late," Kylie said as she hurried through the back door. "Ben wanted to show Charlotte the scan of her baby sister."

"You're having a girl!" Paris left the list on the work table and hugged Kylie. "That's so exciting."

"Just think of all the cute outfits you can dress her in," Jackie said as she gave her boss another hug. "Was everything all right?"

"We're growing a healthy little girl. The only thing I need to watch is my blood pressure. The doctor wants me to work fewer hours for the rest of my pregnancy."

That didn't surprise Paris. Kylie worked long hours and hardly ever took a day off. "Jackie and I can spend more time here."

Kylie sat at their workroom table. "I'm not sure that will help." Gratefully, she took the cup Jackie handed to her.

"It's the special blend of berry tea you like."

"Thanks. It smells delicious." Taking a small sip, she sighed. "This is exactly what I need. While we were waiting for Charlotte, I looked at our bookings for the next six months. I don't know what I was thinking when I agreed to provide the flowers for so many events."

Paris sat beside her. "You have a successful business. Everyone wants Blooming Lovely to make floral arrangements for their special occasions."

"And our prices are much better than any of the florists in Polson." Jackie left a cup of coffee on the table for Paris before pulling out a stool for herself. "I looked at some websites the other day. I was shocked at what other florists are charging."

Kylie wrapped her hands around her cup. "They might have higher costs they need to cover. If I didn't own this store, I'd have to charge more, too."

"Well, I'm glad we can keep the prices of our flowers affordable. Without the extra business it's created, you might not have asked Paris and me to help you."

Paris frowned. "Are you thinking of canceling some of the events we've booked?"

"It's one option," Kylie said slowly. "Between Blooming Lovely and what you do for the Christmas Shop, neither of you have much free time. We'll be okay for the next few months. But, after that, I might have to give up work completely. Unless I can find another florist, we'll have to cancel some bookings or ask another company to provide the flowers."

Paris understood why her boss felt that way, but asking another company to work with their clients seemed like a giant step backward. "What if our customers don't come back? They could ask the new company to provide the flowers for other events they're hosting."

"That's a risk I'll have to take. I'm really sorry I can't work as many hours as we need."

"Don't be silly," Jackie said. "Your health is more important than anything else."

Paris thought about the people whose events would be affected if Kylie wasn't here to help. Even choosing which events to cancel would be difficult—especially in a small town where everyone knew each other.

Kylie left her cup on the table. "Would you like to see the ultrasound photos of our baby?"

With an excited nod, Jackie moved closer. "Can you tell who she looks like?"

"Ben said she has my nose and chin, but I have no idea why he thinks that."

Paris stood beside her two best friends and studied the images. She smiled when she realized what the baby was doing. "Is she sucking her thumb?"

"She is," Kylie placed her hand on her baby bump. "I can't wait to meet her. She was jumping around like a jellybean during the scan."

"She can't sit still, just like her mom," Jackie said with a grin. "You have a beautiful baby girl."

"And two friends who are happy to babysit whenever you need a break," Paris added. "Don't worry about the events we've booked. We'll find a way to get through the next few months."

"I hope so." Kylie looked sadly at Paris and Jackie. "I didn't think I'd have to cut back my hours."

"It's only for a little while." Paris gave Kylie another hug. "We're a team. We'll make it work."

As they admired the pictures of Kylie and Ben's baby, Paris knew everything would be okay. Kylie had worked hard to build Blooming Lovely into a successful business. Their clients would understand if they had to find another florist to make their bouquets and flower arrangements—especially when a new baby was involved.

RICHARD PARKED his truck outside The Welcome Center and rubbed his right leg. After a long day at work, he was glad to almost be home.

Looking across the parking lot, he smiled at the ocean-themed mural he'd created with his son. Before they'd joined the painting project, a row of uninspiring concrete garages separated The Welcome Center from the tiny home village. Working with the village's residents, they'd brought color and life to this side of the property.

The sense of belonging the project gave him was a stark contrast to how he'd felt when he arrived in Sapphire Bay. Emotionally and physically broken after his time in the army, he'd traveled here with his son, four suitcases, and a life that was the complete opposite of everything he'd imagined.

"Good afternoon, Mr. Dawkins."

Richard sighed. Only one person called him Mr. Dawkins, and he tried to stay away from her. Not that he'd had much luck. Sapphire Bay was so small that it was impossible to hide from anyone.

His eyebrows rose when he saw what Paris was wearing. "Let me guess. You're going for a 1950s rockabilly look."

Placing her hands on her pink polka dot skirt, she twisted left and then right. The petticoats under the skirt swished back and forth. "You're getting better. I thought about wearing my Marilyn Munroe dress, but Jackie thought it might be too much."

After seeing some of the outfits she wore, he'd probably agree with Jackie. Paris was like a chameleon, wearing clothes that were as over-the-top as her personality. "Why did you want to dress like Marilyn Munroe?"

"I'm looking after Natalie's art class. We're studying pop culture."

He must have spent too much time around her because he knew exactly what she meant. "And Andy Warhol created a famous painting of Marilyn Munroe."

"Exactly. Are you visiting The Welcome Center or going to the tiny home village?"

"The Welcome Center. Jack's writing class has nearly finished."

Paris lifted the strap of her pink handbag onto her shoulder. "I'll walk with you."

He wasn't sure that was a good idea. Whenever he saw her, one of them usually said something that offended the other. They were better staying apart and saying as little to each other as possible.

"Is Jack enjoying the after-school writing class?"

Richard nodded. At least discussing his son was a safe, neutral topic. "He is. Katie's a great tutor."

"Have you read her latest children's book? It's amazing."

"I'm reading it to Jack at the moment. Why are you tutoring the students in Natalie's art class?"

"She had to fly to Washington, D.C. to open her next exhibition."

"Teaching her class is a lot different from working in the flower shop."

Paris frowned. "You don't think I can do it?"

He could have kicked himself. "I didn't say that."

"Of course, you didn't. But you were thinking it." In true Paris form, she lengthened her stride and stalked away from him.

Richard ran his hand around the back of his neck. He'd met Paris a year ago at a fundraiser for the tiny home village. When he'd spoken to her, warning bells had flashed inside his head. She'd asked too many questions, seen far too much of the man he didn't want to remember. Each time he met her, he tried to figure out why they rubbed each other the wrong way. And, each time, he came away with nothing.

But not being able to understand her wasn't an excuse to make her feel bad.

He caught up to her as she was about to enter the center. "The students are lucky to have you helping them."

"*Now* you say something nice."

"I was surprised you're tutoring the class, that's all."

Paris sighed. "You don't know anything about me, so why should it surprise you?"

He crossed his arms in front of his chest. Most people were intimidated by his height and size, but not Paris. She stood her ground, making up for the difference in their builds by sheer personality. "I didn't know you could paint."

"I can't, but I did some art history papers at UCLA. Natalie wants her students to combine the screen-printing technique she showed them with a pop culture design. I'm supervising the class and answering their questions."

"That sounds interesting. I'm sure you'll do a great job."

"If that's an apology, thank you." She glanced at her watch. "I have to go. Otherwise, everyone will arrive before I do."

"And I'd better find Jack. He'll be wondering where I am."

In silence, they walked into the center and went their separate ways. As he waited with the other parents, he wondered what was wrong with him. With her sparkling blue eyes and jet-black hair, Paris was one of the most attractive women he'd ever met. Whenever he met someone who knew her, they described her as friendly and helpful. So, what was his problem?

"Dad!" Jack rushed out of a meeting room. "You're not going to believe what happened. Chandler vomited all over Mrs. Campbell. The smell was so bad we had to go to a different room."

"I hope Chandler's feeling better."

"He will be. Peggy-Anne said someone dared him to eat worms. Do you want to read my story when we get home?"

Richard took Jack's backpack out of his hands. "Sounds great." With his eight-year-old son chatting beside him, he followed the other parents into the foyer. The flash of a bright pink skirt farther down the corridor caught his eye. His heart sank.

He was tired, hungry, and guilty of thinking the worst of a woman who'd never harmed anyone. He couldn't have started the evening off worse if he'd tried.

THE FOLLOWING MORNING, Paris carried a box of flowers into Blooming Lovely. "He's so annoying. Each time I meet him, he says something that makes my blood boil."

Jackie opened a box she'd already brought inside. "He could be insecure."

"I don't think so. Richard's built like a big, bushy lumberjack, and he's taller than most men in Sapphire Bay. *And* he's a construction foreman at the old steamboat museum."

"Even big men have issues."

Carefully, Paris placed a dozen pale yellow roses on the counter. "As far as I can tell, the only issue he has, is with me."

Jackie grinned. "That would be a first. Our customers adore you, and Mr. Murray calls you his sweetheart."

"I don't mind what Mr. Murray calls me. He's ninety-four and thinks everyone's wonderful. Richard could learn a thing or two from him."

"You want your arch enemy to call you his sweetheart?"

"I'd sooner he didn't call me anything." She glanced at her watch and frowned. "We'd better bring the rest of the flowers inside. I need to make a special order before we open."

"And I promised Kylie I'd change the window display. I can't believe it's nearly Valentine's Day."

Neither could Paris. Each year seemed to go faster than the last. She looked around the workroom as they carried more boxes into Blooming Lovely. It was like an Aladdin's cave of gift-wrapping paper, glittery boxes, and flowers in all shapes and colors. "I don't know what I would have done if Kylie hadn't offered me this job."

"Neither do I, although I suspect Pastor John had a lot to do with us being here. Do you think Kylie will have to reduce our hours?"

Paris had wondered the same thing. "I asked her that yesterday. She doesn't think that will happen. All it will mean is we don't have to work seven days a week."

"I wouldn't want to be the person who tells our clients we can't provide the flowers for their special occasions."

"Neither would I." Paris opened the last box of flowers. "At least Valentine's Day won't be affected."

Jackie picked up a red rose and grinned. "Regardless of what Kylie does, Cupid will never stop creating happily ever afters in Sapphire Bay."

"As long as he stays away from me, he can do whatever he wants."

"For someone who loves Valentine's Day, that doesn't sound very romantic."

"I prefer to watch everyone else enjoy the day." Paris collected the paperwork from each box. "Can you hand me the list of orders we need to make?"

Jackie reached for the clipboard. "Just because you've had some horrible experiences with men, it doesn't mean they're all bad."

"That's what I used to tell myself, but it didn't make any difference. I have some kind of defect that makes me date the wrong people. I'm much happier on my own."

"I don't believe you."

Paris grinned. "You don't have to. Can you pass me the box beside you? I need the lilies for a bouquet."

"You can change the subject as often as you like but, one day, you'll meet an amazing man who will sweep you off your feet."

Picking up a knife, Paris cut through the tape holding the box together. The likelihood of that happening was a million to one. Especially when her superpower was pushing people away.

Click HERE to buy from Leeanna's Store and SAVE!

Or click HERE to purchase from other retailers.

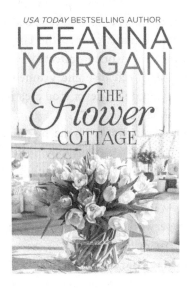

ENJOY MORE BOOKS BY LEEANNA MORGAN

Montana Brides:

Click here to buy from Leeanna's Store and SAVE!

Or from other retailers here:

Book 1: Forever Dreams (Gracie and Trent)

Book 2: Forever in Love (Amy and Nathan)

Book 3: Forever After (Nicky and Sam)

Book 4: Forever Wishes (Erin and Jake)

Book 5: Forever Santa (A Montana Brides Christmas Novella)

Book 6: Forever Cowboy (Emily and Alex)

Book 7: Forever Together (Kate and Dan)

Book 8: Forever and a Day (Sarah and Jordan)

The Bridesmaids Club:

Click here to buy from Leeanna's Store and SAVE!

Or from other retailers here:

Book 1: All of Me (Tess and Logan)

Book 2: Loving You (Annie and Dylan)

Book 3: Head Over Heels (Sally and Todd)

Book 4: Sweet on You (Molly and Jacob)

Emerald Lake:

Click here to buy from Leeanna's Store and SAVE!

Or from other retailers here:

Book 1: Sealed with a Kiss (Rachel and John)

Book 2: Playing for Keeps (Sophie and Ryan)

Book 3: Crazy Love (Holly and Daniel)

Book 4: One And Only (Elizabeth and Blake)

The Protectors:

Click here to buy from Leeanna's Store and SAVE!

Or from other retailers here:

Book 1: Safe Haven (Hayley and Tank)

Book 2: Just Breathe (Kelly and Tanner)

Book 3: Always (Mallory and Grant)

Book 4: The Promise (Ashley and Matthew)

Montana Promises:

Click here to buy from Leeanna's Store and SAVE!

Or from other retailers here:

Book 1: Coming Home (Mia and Stan)

Book 2: The Gift (Hannah and Brett)

Book 3: The Wish (Claire and Jason)

Book 4: Country Love (Becky and Sean)

Sapphire Bay:

Click here to buy from Leeanna's Store and SAVE!

Or from other retailers here:

Book 1: Falling For You (Natalie and Gabe)

Book 2: Once In A Lifetime (Sam and Caleb)

Book 3: A Christmas Wish (Megan and William)

Book 4: Before Today (Brooke and Levi)

Book 5: The Sweetest Thing (Cassie and Noah)

Book 6: Sweet Surrender (Willow and Zac)

Santa's Secret Helpers:

Click here to buy from Leeanna's Store and SAVE!

Or from other retailers here:

Book 1: Christmas On Main Street (Emma and Jack)

Book 2: Mistletoe Madness (Kylie and Ben)

Book 3: Silver Bells (Bailey and Steven)

Book 4: The Santa Express (Shelley and John)

Book 5: Endless Love (The Jones Family)

Return To Sapphire Bay:

Click here to buy from Leeanna's Store and SAVE!

Or from other retailers here:

Book 1: The Lakeside Inn (Penny and Wyatt)

Book 2: Summer At Lakeside (Diana and Ethan)

Book 3: A Lakeside Thanksgiving (Barbara and Theo)

Book 4: Christmas At Lakeside (Katie and Peter)

The Cottages on Anchor Lane:

Click here to buy from Leeanna's Store and SAVE!

Or from other retailers here:

Book 1: The Flower Cottage (Paris and Richard)

Book 2: The Starlight Café (Andrea and David)

Book 3: The Cozy Quilt Shop (Shona and Joseph)

Book 4: A Stitch in Time (Jackie and Aidan)

Love on Anchor Lane:

Click here to buy from Leeanna's Store and SAVE!

Or from other retailers here:

Made in the USA
Middletown, DE
04 June 2024